PRASE FOR *THE T*

"A potent, vaporous fever dream; a meditation on truth, lie, illusion, and time that floats like an aromatic haze through Herzog's vivid reconstruction of Onoda's war. . . . Hofmann's resonant translation conveys the portentous shimmer of Herzog's voice."

—*The New York Times Book Review*

"[A] wondrous first novel." —*The New Yorker*

"A spare and lyric tale . . . In his feverish search for ecstatic truths, Herzog has given readers a portal into human folly, self-discipline, and domination—surely his life's work." —*The Washington Post*

"As profound and thought-provoking as the best of his films, Herzog's *The Twilight World* delivers as a superb yet painful parable on the fleeting nature of purpose." —*San Francisco Chronicle*

"From the true story of a WWII soldier who kept up the fight until 1974, legendary filmmaker Herzog distills a brooding, poetic novella. . . . Herzog, ever in pursuit of deeper truths, sees in Onoda's predicament an all-too-ordinary tendency to subordinate facts to master narratives." —*Booklist*

"There's an element of the romantic as well in Herzog's jungle survival tales, where the universe boils down to individuals wrestling with nature and being shaped by it in turn. . . . This is why Herzog loves the jungle, for its capacity to show us at our most abject and our most inspiring." —*The New Republic*

"Filmmaker Herzog draws on the true story of a Japanese officer who patrolled the Filipino jungle for nearly three decades after WWII, unaware the war had ended, in his fascinating debut novel. . . . Onoda shares with the director's filmic protagonists a fierce will and singular perspective. This will whet the reader's appetite for a film version." —*Publishers Weekly*

PENGUIN BOOKS

THE TWILIGHT WORLD

Werner Herzog was born in Munich on September 5, 1942. He made his first film in 1961 at the age of nineteen. Since then he has produced, written, and directed more than seventy feature and documentary films, including *Aguirre, the Wrath of God*; *Nosferatu*; *Fitzcarraldo*; *Little Dieter Needs to Fly*; *My Best Fiend*; *Grizzly Man*; *Encounters at the End of the World*; and *Cave of Forgotten Dreams*. Herzog has published more than a dozen books of prose and directed as many operas. He lives in Munich and Los Angeles.

Michael Hofmann is a German-born poet who writes in English. He has translated the works of Bertolt Brecht, Franz Kafka, Hans Fallada, and Joseph Roth, and teaches at the University of Florida in Gainesville.

THE
TWILIGHT
WORLD

WERNER HERZOG

TRANSLATED BY
MICHAEL HOFMANN

PENGUIN BOOKS

PENGUIN BOOKS
An imprint of Penguin Random House LLC
penguinrandomhouse.com

First published in the United States of America by Penguin Press,
an imprint of Penguin Random House LLC, 2022
Published in Penguin Books 2023

Originally published in German as *Das Dämmern der Welt*
by Carl Hanser Verlag GmbH & Co. KG, München

ISBN 9780593490280 (paperback)

THE LIBRARY OF CONGRESS HAS CATALOGED THE HARDCOVER EDITION AS FOLLOWS:
Names: Herzog, Werner, 1942– author. | Hofmann, Michael,
    1957 August 25–translator.
Title: The twilight world / Werner Herzog ; translated by Michael Hofmann.
Other titles: Dämmern der Welt. English
Description: New York : Penguin Press, 2022. | "Originally published
    in German as Das Dämmern der Welt by Carl Hanser Verlag
    GmbH & Co. KG, München."
Identifiers: LCCN 2021042961 (print) | LCCN 2021042962 (ebook) |
    ISBN 9780593490266 (hardcover) | ISBN 9780593490273 (ebook)
Subjects: LCSH: Onoda, Hiroo. | Japan. Rikugun—Biography. | Soldiers—
    Japan—Biography. | Guerrilla warfare—Philippines—Lubang Islands. |
    World War, 1939–1945—Philippines—Lubang Islands. | World War,
    1939–1945—Armistices.
Classification: LCC DS890.O53 H4713 2022 (print) |
    LCC DS890.O53 (ebook) | DDC 940.54/8252—dc23/eng/20211104
LC record available at https://lccn.loc.gov/2021042961
LC ebook record available at https://lccn.loc.gov/2021042962

Printed in the United States of America
10 9 8 7 6 5 4 3 2 1

Book design by Daniel Lagin

Most details are factually correct; some are not. What was important to the author was something other than accuracy, some essence he thought he glimpsed when he encountered the protagonist of this story.

THE TWILIGHT WORLD

n 1997, I was in Tokyo to direct the opera *Chushingura*. Shigeaki Saegusa, the composer, had long pressed me to take on the world premiere of this work. *Chushingura* is the most Japanese of all Japanese stories: there is a religious ceremony impending; the preparations are in hand; in the course of these, a feudal lord is provoked and insulted; he draws his sword. As punishment for his sacrilege, he is made to commit ritual suicide, seppuku. Two years later, forty-seven of his retainers avenge him by ambushing and killing the man who insulted their master. They know that they must die for such an action. That same day, all forty-seven kill themselves.

Saegusa is a widely respected composer in Japan. At the time of the production, he had his own TV show, and people knew about the work we were doing. In the evening, some of us would have dinner together at a long table. Saegusa came late one day, and in a state of high excitement. "Herzog-san," he said. His Highness, the Emperor had indicated he would receive me to a private audience, if I wasn't too busy with the upcoming premiere. I replied: "My goodness, I have no idea what I would talk about with the Emperor; it would be nothing but banalities." I could feel my wife Lena's nails digging into my palm, but it was too late. I had declined.

It was a faux pas, so awful, so catastrophic that I wish to this day that the earth had swallowed me up. Around the table, everyone present froze. No one breathed. All eyes were fixed on their plates, no one looked at me, a protracted silence made the room shudder. It felt to me as though the whole of Japan had stopped breathing. Just then, into the silence, a voice inquired: "Well, if not the Emperor, whom would you like to meet?" I instantly replied: "Onoda."

"Onoda? Onoda?"

"Yes," I replied. "Hiroo Onoda." And a week later, I met him.

Lubang, a Path in the Jungle

The night coils in fever dreams. No sooner awake than with an awful shudder, the landscape reveals itself as a durable daytime version of the same nightmare, crackling and flickering like loosely connected neon tubes. From daybreak the jungle has twitched in the ritual tortures of elec tricity. Rain. The storm is so distant that its thunder is not yet audible. A dream? Is it a dream? A wide path, on either side dense underbrush, rotting mulch on the ground, the leaves dripping. The jungle remains stiff, patient, humble, until the office of the rain has been celebrated.

Then this, as though I'd been there myself. Sounds of voices in the distance; happy cries coming ever nearer. From the bodiless mist of the jungle a body acquires form. A young

Filipino man comes hurrying along the path, down the slight incline. Curious, as he runs, in one hand he holds up over his head the remnants of an umbrella, now nothing but a wire skeleton and shreds of cloth, in the other a bolo knife. Close behind him is a woman with an infant on her arm, followed by seven or eight other villagers. What has provoked the joyous excitement is not evident. They hurry by, then nothing happens. The steady drip, drip from the trees, the quiet path.

A path, just a jungle footpath. And yet, immediately in front of me, on the right-hand side, a stir passes through a few of the moldering leaves. What was that? Another moment of stillness. Then a section of the wall of leaves at eye level in front of me, that too begins to move. Slowly, terribly slowly, a green man takes form. Is it a ghost? The thing I have been watching all along without recognizing it is a Japanese soldier. Hiroo Onoda. Even if I had known exactly where he was standing, I would not have seen him, so consummate is his camouflage. He peels the wet leaves off his legs, then the green twigs he has carefully fastened to his body. He reaches into the thicket for his rifle, beside which he has concealed his camouflaged rucksack. I see a military man in his early fifties; a wiry build; every movement exaggeratedly circumspect. His uniform is made of sewn-together scraps; the butt of his rifle is wound around with tree bark. He listens intently, then disappears silently after the villagers. Ahead of me is the clay path, still the same, but new now, different, full of secrets. Was it a dream?

The path, a little lower now, has widened out at this point. The rain is no more than a trickle. Onoda studies the footprints in the clay, listening all the time, constantly on the alert. His lively eyes swivel in every direction. The birds have struck up, calmly, as though to assure him that danger is a word in a dictionary now, a mysterious condition of the landscape. The humming of the insects is regular. I start to hear with Onoda's ears that their humming is not aggressive, is not troubled. From afar the pouring of a stream, even though I have yet to see a stream, as though I were, like Onoda, beginning to translate sounds.

Lubang, Wakayama Tributary

At this point, the clerestory of the forest has overgrown a narrow rivulet. Clear water pours over flat stones. A second stream joins it from the left, descending from steep wooded hills. Past the confluence of the two, the landscape widens out, flattens. Bamboo, palms, tall rushes. At the confluence itself there is a flat sandbank. Onoda crosses the sand walking backward, leaving traces to mislead a possible pursuer. Through the slowly swaying rushes he can make out a small Japanese flag. Onoda cautiously raises his field glasses, worn and marked by so many years in the jungle. Are they in fact still field glasses? Weren't the prisms long ago attacked by a mold? Or is Onoda impossible to imagine without his field glasses? The flag flaps a little in the afternoon breeze.

Its fabric is so new that the creases where it was folded are still clearly discernible.

There is a tent beside the flag. It, too, fresh from the factory, the sort of tent trippers might use for a weekend outing. Onoda cautiously straightens up. He sees a young man squatting on the ground, facing away, trying to get a fire going in a camp stove. Apparently alone. A nylon rucksack in the mouth of the tent. When the young man turns to reach for it to make a windbreak next to the cooker, his face shows: it is Norio Suzuki.

Onoda leaps forth from his ambush. Suzuki is rigid with terror, sees the rifle pointing at him. It takes him a moment to recover the power of speech.

"I'm Japanese," he says, "I'm Japanese."

"On your knees," commands Onoda. Suzuki slowly gets down on his knees.

"Take your shoes off. Throw them away as far as you can."

Suzuki follows the command, he is trembling so hard he has trouble with the laces.

"I'm unarmed," he says. "This is just a kitchen knife."

Onoda pays no regard to the knife on the ground. Suzuki carefully pushes it away.

"Are you Onoda? Hiroo Onoda?"

"Yes. Lieutenant Onoda. That's me."

Onoda points his rifle at the middle of Suzuki's chest, stoical, opaque. Now animation comes over Suzuki's features.

"Am I dreaming? Am I really seeing what I'm seeing?"

Daylight has given way to evening. Onoda and Suzuki are squatting by the fire a little way away from Suzuki's tent. Nocturnal crickets start their thrumming. Onoda has taken up a position from where he is able to survey the surroundings with his continually swiveling regard. He is suspicious, alert, his rifle still pointed in the general direction of Suzuki. It seems they must have been speaking for a while. After a pause, Suzuki takes up the conversation.

"How could I be an American agent? I'm only twenty-two years old."

Onoda is not impressed. "When I came here at the beginning of the war, I was one year older than you. Any effort to deflect me from my mission was the work of enemy agents."

"I am not your enemy. My only purpose was to meet you."

"Men in civilian clothes came ashore on the island. Men in disguise. They all wanted the same thing: to kill me or take me prisoner. I have survived a hundred and eleven ambushes. I have been repeatedly attacked. I can no longer count how many times I was fired upon. Every human being on this island is my enemy."

Suzuki has no answer. Onoda looks off in the direction of the last light in the sky.

"Do you know what a fired bullet looks like, in light like this?"

"No. I can't say I do."

"It has a bluish glow, almost like tracer."

"Really?"

"You can see it coming toward you, if it's fired from far enough away."

"And you weren't hit?" Suzuki asks, in perplexity.

"I would have been hit. I turned aside, and the bullet went past me."

"Do bullets whistle as they fly?"

"No, but they make a sort of vibration. A low buzz."

Suzuki is impressed.

Another voice joins in. There's a distant flickering in the night sky. The new voice is singing something.

"Who's there?" Suzuki can't make anyone out.

"That would be Shimada, Corporal Shimada. He died here."

"But wasn't that in the middle fifties? I read about it. Everyone in Japan knows about it."

"He died nineteen years, nine months, and fourteen days ago. We were ambushed here, by the Wakayama tributary."

"Wakayama?" asks Suzuki. "Sounds Japanese."

"Right at the beginning of our mission on Lubang, my battalion chose this name for the tributary, in honor of my native prefecture, Wakayama."

The crickets are louder, filling the scene with their noise. The conversation is all theirs now. Suzuki thinks for a long time. Finally, all the crickets scream out at once, in some collective indignation.

"Onoda-san?"

"Lieutenant."

"Lieutenant, we seem to be going around in circles."

Suzuki is silent. Onoda prods Suzuki in the chest with the rifle, not threateningly, but to make sure he keeps the fire going.

"If you're no enemy agent, who are you?"

"My name is Norio Suzuki. I used to be a student at Tokyo University."

"Used to be?"

"I quit."

"No student at the best university in the country quits."

"I was bothered because I could see my whole future mapped out ahead of me, every step of the way to retirement and pension."

"Well?" Onoda doesn't understand.

"I wanted a couple of years of freedom, before I sacrificed my life to being a businessman."

"Well?"

"I started to travel. I hitchhiked. I've been to forty countries."

"What is this—hitchhiking?"

"Waving to cars, hoping they pick you up and take you wherever they're going. No special destination. Until I got there."

"Where?"

"Truly, I had three aims. The first one was to find you, Lieutenant Onoda."

"No one finds me. In twenty-nine years no one has found me."

Suzuki feels encouraged.

"I have been here for under two days, and I have found you."

"*I* stumbled upon you, I found you. You didn't find me. If you hadn't been so reckless with regard to danger, I would probably have killed you."

Suzuki has not expected this. He is silent.

"And what were your two other objectives?"

"The yeti—"

"Who?"

"Sometimes called the abominable snowman. A terrible creature in the Himalayas, covered in fur. They have found traces of him, he does exist. And then the giant panda in its natural habitat in the mountains in China. In that order: Onoda, yeti, panda."

For the first time, there's a flicker of amusement on Onoda's face. He nods to Suzuki, go on, don't stop.

Suzuki feels encouraged. "The war ended twenty-nine years ago."

Utter expressionless incomprehension from Onoda.

"That can't be."

"Japan capitulated in August 1945."

"The war is not over. A couple of days ago, I saw an American aircraft carrier, accompanied by a destroyer and a frigate."

"Heading East, I expect," says Suzuki.

"Don't try to trick me. I see what I see."

Suzuki remains insistent. "Lieutenant, the Americans have their biggest naval base in Subic Bay. All their navy ships are refitted and equipped there."

"The Bay of Manila? That's only ninety kilometers away."

"Yes."

"That base existed at the beginning of the war. How do American ships now come and use it?"

"The US and the Philippines are allies."

"What about the planes, the fighters and bombers, I see them all the time?"

"They're headed for Clark Air Base, North of the Bay of Manila. With such huge forces, Lieutenant, why wouldn't the enemy simply overrun Lubang? After all, Lubang controls access to the Bay of Manila."

"I'm not privy to the enemy's plans."

"There are no more plans, the war is over."

Onoda struggles with himself for a moment. Then slowly he gets to his feet, takes a step toward Suzuki, and presses the muzzle of his rifle against his forehead.

"All right, tell me the truth. The time has come."

"Lieutenant, I am not afraid of dying. But it would be miserable to be killed for telling the truth."

The night becomes the longest night, a shock for Onoda, who is torn this way and that between doubt and acceptance. There is no visible sign of this, his face remains stony. Atomic bombs dropped on two Japanese cities, a hundred thousand dead just like that? Something about the energy released from the splitting of atoms, made into a weapon. How? Suzuki lacks the technological understanding to explain it. Other countries had by now also acquired this thing, this atomic bomb. The existing arsenal was so great that it could kill every inhabitant of the earth not just once or twice, but 1,240 times. For Onoda, this is not compatible with the logic of any war he can conceive of, not even in the future.

What had happened after—allegedly—the two bombs had fallen on Japan is what Onoda wants to know. It was August 1945. Japan had capitulated unconditionally. The Emperor had addressed his people over the wireless. No one had ever heard his voice before. He had taken the opportunity to declare that he was not a god. Such a pronouncement is so inconceivable to Onoda that he takes it as final proof that Suzuki has come on a mission to deceive him. He drills the muzzle of the rifle between Suzuki's eyes.

"No. The truth is that the war has gone on. Perhaps it just carried on elsewhere."

But Suzuki remains adamant. "In the West, Germany lost. They surrendered before the Japanese did."

"No," says Onoda, "the war went on, and it went on in the West as well. What I saw is proof."

"Proof? What do you mean, 'proof'?"

"I saw wave after wave of American warplanes flying overhead. Right here, going that way, West."

"When was this?"

"It went on for years."

"Beginning when?"

"In 1950. Also bombers and troop transporters, naval ships."

"That was the Korean War."

"Korean War? What Korean War? Korea belongs to us."

"The Communists threw out the Japanese. Then the US started a war with the Communists."

"And America evidently lost."

"Half won, half lost. Today, Korea has been partitioned. There is a Communist North and a Capitalist South."

Onoda is finding it difficult to process so much information.

"But those waves of warplanes, they never stopped."

"What warplanes? When?"

"Always going West. American bombers directly overhead. More and more all the time. From 1965, in vast formations. Whole convoys of ships, bigger all the time, more and more of them. And you're trying to tell me, the war has ended?"

"That was the Vietnam War."

"The what?"

Onoda leans back. The night is long. The crickets, not caring about war or peace, or who gets to name wars and for what reason, intensify their monotonous screaming, this is their war, perhaps also their peace negotiations, equally unbeknownst to us. The moon. The early light of the coming day makes it still paler, a heavenly body without any deeper meaning that has been around for millions of years before there were any humans.

As though following some silent understanding, Onoda and Suzuki look up at it at one and the same time. "Men have landed on the moon," Suzuki says softly, as though reluctant to say too many shocking things too quickly.

"When? How?"

"In the last five years. The crews flew in rockets and space capsules. I'm loath to say so, but the astronauts were Americans, our former foes."

"America is still our enemy."

"Not really. They even attended our Olympic Games."

"I know about those Games," says Onoda.

"How so?" asks Suzuki.

"Enemy agents left out copies of carefully fabricated Japanese newspapers in various places all over the island. Some parts of them even looked credible, but the only point of them was to lure me out of the jungle." Onoda stops, considers. "I will carry on with my war. I have been fighting for thirty years already, and I have many more years left in me."

"But those facts I was able to tell you about—"

"I'll think about it," Onoda interrupts him.

"What would it take to make you end your campaign?" Suzuki asks softly.

Onoda thinks about it.

"All those leaflets dropped from airplanes calling on me to surrender—they were all fakes, I can prove it."

He says it more to himself than to his unexpected visitor.

"There is only one condition on which I would surrender. Only one."

"And what would that be?" asks Suzuki.

"If one of my superior officers were to come here and give me the order to cease hostilities, then I would surrender. But only then."

Suzuki straightaway takes up the thought.

"Let me try to get someone here. Though admittedly any officer I found would first have to be reactivated. With the new constitution Japan only has a very small army, and exclusively for purposes of self-defense."

Suzuki starts doing sums.

"I could be back in Tokyo inside two or three days. Then let's say another ten days to arrange everything. I could be here again in three weeks."

Onoda reflects quickly. "That sounds possible."

Suzuki hurries: "What do you say to the following suggestion? We meet here again in exactly this spot. I'll bring one of your former superiors. No Filipino troops. No one else. Just him and me."

Onoda's tone waxes formal. "I accept. But if you try to trick me, I will open fire without warning on you and anyone else with you."

No handshake, just a curt bow. The men do not touch. Suzuki feels emboldened. "Would you mind if I took a picture of you?"

"No," says Onoda. "Only if we're both in it together."

Suzuki digs out his camera. Because he doesn't have a tripod, he places it on his rucksack. He jumps back to Onoda, who is squatting on the ground six feet away.

"There'll be a flash any second. You probably have no idea what a sensation the picture will be all over the world."

"Hold my rifle," says Onoda. "That can be proof that I trust you."

Both men are bathed in the flash. Onoda frowns at Suzuki.

"Partly anyway. Partly."

Lubang Airfield

December 1944

The airfield is small, with cracked, washed-out asphalt that hasn't been patched in years. There are a few single-story buildings in the background, rusted tin roofs, all in varying stages of neglect. On the other side of the strip is the open sea, with the small island of Cabra to the North, barely visible in the haze. A Japanese troop transporter is at anchor just offshore. Small, clumsy landing craft are ferrying Japanese troops out to it. A battalion of tired Japanese soldiers has marched up in formation. Their uniforms have not had the jungle fully washed out of them, a few of the men are wearing rubber boots they must have got from the locals. As they march toward the landing craft, they pass the wreckage of two fighter planes that has been cleared off the runway.

Major Taniguchi and Onoda, thirty years his junior, in the shade of an empty hangar. Onoda, standing at attention, is receiving orders from his superior officer. The Major is formal.

"Lieutenant Onoda, I have orders for you from headquarters." Onoda stands a little more stiffly.

"Yes, sir, Lieutenant Onoda at your command."

"You are the only man here who has had training in secret warfare, in guerrilla tactics."

"Sir. Major."

"These are your orders. As soon as our troops have been withdrawn from Lubang, it is your duty to hold the island until the Imperial Army's return. You are to defend its territory by guerrilla tactics, at all costs. You will have to make your own decisions. No one will give you orders. You must be self-reliant. Henceforth there are no more rules, you make the rules."

Onoda is impassive. "Yes, sir. Major."

"There is only one rule," Taniguchi continues. "You are forbidden to die by your own hand. In the event of your capture by the enemy, you are to give them all the misleading information you can."

The Major beckons Onoda into the almost cleared hangar. Everything here looks temporary. No Japanese planes being refitted, just an untidy heap of provisions and military equipment. The two officers walk up to a wall that still has several maps pinned to it; one is of the island of Lubang. The Major points to it.

"You have two immediate tasks, right now, even before the evacuation is complete. One: all explosives still on the island are placed under your control. With them you are to destroy this airfield. Two: with any remaining explosive, you are to destroy the landing pier at Tilik. These are the two prime access points to the enemy."

Onoda studies the map. The island is an oblong shape, some twenty-five kilometers in length. In its central section it is hilly and overgrown with jungle, without any roads or settlements. Facing Tilik, and not far from the town of Lubang to the North, lies the Bay of Manila, some eighty kilometers distant. The narrow southwestern tip of the island, across the hills, is flat, but again without any discernible roads. All there is is one small village: Looc.

Onoda asks: "How many men will I have under my command, sir?"

"We will put together a troop for you, Onoda," says the Major. "Admittedly, there won't be anyone among them who is an expert in secret warfare. And no one will know about your orders. In this type of warfare, there is no prospect of medals."

"I don't fight for medals."

The men don't speak.

"Sir?" asks Onoda.

"If you have questions, ask now. This is your chance."

"Will my responsibility be confined to Lubang, or do I have a wider sphere of operations? The small outlying islands— Cabra, Ambil, Golo?"

"Why do you ask?"

"Major, the island is not especially big, and it's two-thirds covered in jungle. It's not much for a guerrilla war."

"Onoda, you should bear in mind that Lubang's strategic significance is all the greater," replies the Major. "When the Imperial Army returns in triumph, we will use it as a launching pad for a great attack on the Bay of Manila. The enemy will have concentrated all its forces there."

Onoda's expression remains opaque.

The Major wants no possibility of misunderstanding. "Your base of operations will be the jungle. Your campaign will be one of attrition. Skirmishes, ambushes, unpredictable attacks. You will be like a ghost, elusive, a continuing nightmare to the enemy. Your war will be without glory."

Lubang

January 1945

Recollections, or maybe dreams, of the ensuing days are foggy, have taken on a life of their own. Scraps of things, subject to alteration and rearrangement, hard to grasp and lacking a scheme, like a tourbillion of dried leaves that nevertheless indicates where it has come from and where it is going. Hence, a truck, confiscated by the Japanese and used only lately for the transport of earth and lumber, crawling along a muddy road. The terrain is flat, it is raining. They are somewhere in the northern part of the island. Wet banana plantations on either side, coconut palms farther off. A couple of water buffalo standing beside a hut roofed with palm fronds, so motionless as though they had been that way for weeks. Onoda and six men are huddled on the bed of the truck under a piece of canvas sheeting, wet, heavy, and sore. Next to Onoda in the scant shelter is Corporal Shimada, a young soldier in his early twenties. Some Filipino villagers stop the truck, ask them to take their sick water buffalo somewhere, but the Japanese refuse.

A munitions dump on the edge of the jungle, just a shed knocked together from sheets of corrugated metal by a handful of men. A powerful wind. At this point the hills begin, densely covered with steaming forest. Japanese soldiers jump off the truck and pull open the gate, which is nothing but a wooden frame filled in with rusty metal sheeting. In the gloaming there are heaps of mortar and artillery shells. A sudden wind gust rips the gate from the soldier's hand and slams it against the building so hard that it breaks apart, and pieces of sheeting fly off. One single piece is left hanging on the frame; it is whistling in the gale.

Onoda is furious, but masters himself. Or is it that this scene has been produced in his memory with the benefit of hindsight? Right next to the munitions are a few beaten-up looking metal barrels. Onoda tests the contents of one with a bamboo probe. "Corporal Shimada, these barrels contain petrol. Petrol and explosives must never be stored together. Who is responsible?"

Shimada shrugs. "No one bothers about those army rules anymore."

Onoda raises his voice, he wants everyone to hear him. "From now on, I'm in charge. We all hold equal responsibility. We are the army."

Shimada looks around. "Sir, I understand. An army of seven."

But it is Shimada, who grew up on a farm, who has a solution for the removal of the heaviest bombs, which weigh half a ton apiece.

"Lieutenant," he assures Onoda, "back home we once pulled a thousand-pound ox out of a bog." Under his instructions, a tree trunk is rapidly converted into a lever, whose pivot is formed by several of the petrol barrels trundled together. A bomb of vast caliber is then raised on the shorter part of the tree trunk and levered up onto the truck bed. Once arrived at the airfield with his load, Onoda straightaway is involved in a confrontation with the commander there, Lieutenant Hayakawa, who is unwilling to let any of his own men help unload the bombs onto the airstrip.

"The withdrawing units," he declares, "require the airstrip for the evacuation of heavy matériel." Hayakawa also wants the airstrip to remain intact until such time as the Imperial Air Forces regain control of the skies. But Onoda, though committed to silence, has his own, secret, orders to follow.

"This airstrip will be taken by the enemy," he says, "unless we comprehensively destroy it. Otherwise they will simply use it against us. Do you understand that the complete evacuation of Lubang has been ordered?"

Hayakawa takes refuge in propaganda: "Our glorious airmen will soon be needing this airfield again. Our withdrawal is temporary and tactical."

LUBANG, TILIK

JANUARY 1945

Restlessness. Darkness. The pier at Tilik extends some seventy meters into the bay. Onoda and his men are busy fixing sticks of dynamite and other explosives to the supports, while overhead Japanese soldiers confused in the darkness are trying to find evacuation vessels. A few flash lights make wild tracks in the night sky. Soldiers jump into fishing boats, which are, however, uncrewed and tied up. Finally, a landing craft picks up a number of the leaderless Japanese troops. The Japanese withdrawal is disorderly in the extreme.

Onoda gives orders that the pier props are to be dynamited every ten meters. Corporal Shimada wires up the explosives with electrical wire, but is sufficiently pragmatic—measure twice, cut once—to double it up with fuse wire because he doesn't trust the electricity supply. He holds a flashlight gripped between his teeth. An officer happens to notice what is going on. He approaches Onoda: "You are dynamiting this pier, is that correct?"

"Captain, that's exactly what I'm doing."

"I want you to desist, and that's an order."

Onoda remains perfectly calm. "I have special orders of my own."

This enrages the officer. "Man, don't you see our troops are using the pier? Tomorrow morning there will be more of them, and we'll be passing through this way for at least two more days. There are units in the interior with which we have lost contact."

Onoda thinks for a moment. "My orders allow me some latitude. But the enemy is on his way. As soon as our men have left the island, I will embark on the work of destruction."

At dawn, Onoda has the truck park on the perimeter of Tilik. He collects everything he needs. Abandoned munitions crates full of bullets, hand grenades, rice sacks with a field kitchen. Next to it a large tent, with all the sides rolled up. There are soldiers lying on simple field beds. Only now does Onoda realize this is a field hospital. A wounded man pulls himself up and asks for some explosives. Many of the men have grave injuries and would rather commit suicide than fall into enemy hands.

"Are you not being evacuated? Who is collecting you?" asks Onoda.

"No one," replies the wounded man.

"No one?"

"We have been abandoned. Yesterday there were two medical orderlies, but they left when darkness fell. They said they had to go and look after some casualties in Tilik, but we happen to know there has been no fighting in or around Tilik for weeks now." In spite of his grave wound, the soldier sits up on his bed. "I know how to set bombs off."

Onoda reflects quickly. "All right, I'll leave you some of our explosives. Are you still able to throw a hand grenade?"

"Leave the explosives by my bed, and I will just pull the pin," the soldier assures him.

From this point, Onoda's memories are blurred. The only clear thing is that he wasn't able to destroy the airfield at Lubang. All the other units are uncooperative, no troops are seconded to him, troops who wouldn't have been his to command, in any case—the radar unit, the ack-ack unit, the ground teams for the planes, the squad responsible for the naval units, who have been left without a CO. Onoda's idea then is to let the enemy destroy the airfield. Together with a few unwilling individuals from the ground team, he drags a couple of shot-up fighter planes onto the runway and crudely fixes them up so that from the air they might appear to be planes all set to go up.

"Our leaders should have developed such strategies long ago," Onoda says.

Lieutenant Hayakawa finds this form of battle unworthy. "I will fight for the honor of our Emperor, and in honorable combat."

"How do you?" Onoda asks. But Hayakawa finds such cowardice undeserving of a reply. In the long years to come, Onoda will repeatedly think about the way creatures defend themselves in nature, how they make themselves invisible like moths taking on the blotches of tree bark, fish whose coloration matches the pebbles on the riverbed, insects that resemble the green leaves of trees, spiders like diabolical harpists plucking irresistible melodies from their strings and thus cause the webs of an enemy species to vibrate just as though an insect had become caught up in them. Consumed by curiosity, the queen spider approaches the web, and her doom. Or the snake whose rattle distracts the rabbit from the mortal danger approaching. The deep-sea fish whose light signal lures smaller fish that thus allow themselves to be trapped. And how do such creatures protect themselves? By playing dead, like the beetle that lies on its back. By the spines of cacti and thorn trees or the quills from animals like the porcupine, the hedgehog, the spiny fish that at the same time are able to inflate themselves to such a degree that they are too big to be swallowed. Safety in poison, as is the case with wasps and snakes and stinging nettles; by shocks, as from the electric eel, and by malodorous secretions, as is the case with skunks; by a thick veil of ink from octopi. Misdirection, ruse, mimicry—all elements that Onoda wants to learn from nature, whether honorable or otherwise. The only criteria are effectiveness in battle and achieving one's objective. Instead of a full-frontal attack with banners waving, he wants to make himself invisible, become an impalpable dream figure, an elusive and deadly mist, a rumor, a report. Through him the jungle is to become more than a jungle, a landscape with a deadly nimbus of sudden demise.

One last time, Onoda and Shimada draw up outside the improvised field hospital in their truck. The situation is as hopeless as ever. The wounded man to whom Onoda gave the hand grenade to set off the munitions is barely conscious. Mute looks follow him from the camp beds. Onoda lines the truck up alongside the hospital. He and Shimada shoulder heavy rucksacks and grab their rifles. Attached to Onoda's webbing belt is a samurai sword that has been in his family since the seventeenth century. Thus far, he has managed to keep it safe wherever he has been posted. The two soldiers salute in the direction of their wounded comrades and silently melt into the hilly jungle that here begins.

Lubang, Jungle

End of January 1945

Onoda and Shimada have camouflaged themselves in a few strips of soiled canvas, and are crouching in thick vegetation on a jungle slope. Night, distant rumble of artillery, and scattered explosions reach them in waves, like the sea rolling up a pebbled beach. Sheaves of tracer fire draw lines in the black air. A great furnace is throbbing, like a great animal breathing fire. Onoda carefully displaces a wet twig. "Tilik. Just as we predicted. It's the invasion."

Shimada hesitates to say it, but from now on everything that is is the truth, even if it can still change and develop a life of its own. "We didn't destroy the pier."

Onoda is silent. "I am filled with shame. But nothing can change the fact."

Shimada tries to say something comforting. "This invasion is so huge, so overwhelming, that we can be sure the Americans would have landed here anyway, pier or no pier, defended by us or not."

The following day Onoda and Shimada climb up to the top of the twin peak. The pale line of the ocean is way below them to their left. Up here, Japanese troops have dug a trench, sufficient protection for a dozen or so troops. A few individuals are lying apathetically on the ground, loused up, disillusioned. A tent has been pitched nearby, but there is no one in it. Ammunition crates are littered about, a ripped open sack of rice, cooking equipment, all with no discernible rhyme or reason.

"Who is in charge here?" Onoda asks.

"We've been left to our own devices. And now I'm going," replies a soldier, and he takes the initiative and clambers out of the trench.

He has a plan too. To head South, to Looc, at the other end of the island. From up here on the mountain, they had seen plenty of movements out at sea, to the East, toward Manila. The enemy had made landfall at Tilik with considerable strength, but all they seemed interested in was the northern part of the island, with the towns of Lubang and Tilik. Onoda, for his part, is certain that the entire island will be taken over.

But the man sets off, and a couple more climb out of the slimy trench and follow him. Onoda can do nothing about it. The soldiers disobey him and march off. The remaining men hunker down still lower in their ditch, avoiding eye contact with Onoda. How do they think they're going to resist? he asks the prone figures. A vast army was about to turn up, with artillery, mortars, and machine guns, not to mention air support from the US Air Forces. One soldier turns to face Onoda: "Not so, sir. The air support will be coming from our own Imperial Air Forces."

Onoda has seen and heard enough. He draws his sword and points in the direction of the jungle. "Follow me. It's your only chance of further resistance. No one will survive up here, and no one at the bottom of the island will survive either."

He burrows into the thickest part of the jungle. Apart from Shimada, no one else follows him. For a moment longer, the leaves continue to rustle, then the green wall has swallowed them up.

Lubang

Time, time and the jungle. The jungle does not recognize time. They are like two alienated siblings who will have nothing to do with each other, who communicate, if at all, only in the form of contempt. Days follow nights, but there are no seasons as such, at the most, months with vast amounts of rain and months with slightly less rain. There is one unvarying constant: everything in the jungle is at pains to strangle everything else in the battle for sunlight. It may be pitch-black at night, but nothing changes the overwhelming, implacable present tense of the jungle. Bird sounds and the shrill of crickets, as though a great locomotive had applied its emergency brakes and were screaking uncontrollably along the rails, for hours and hours, without stopping. Then, as though under the baton of a phantom conductor, they suddenly fall silent, all at once; the choir gasps and holds its breath. Onoda and Shimada duck simultaneously. The birds, too, are silent. A warning? Some approaching danger? Nothing stirs. Then the mighty shrill of the crickets resumes, again all at once, synchronized to a fraction of a second.

Shimada risks a whispered communication. "I know where the rice depot is."

"On Snake Mountain," hazards Onoda.

"No, some way from there, at Hill 500." Shimada knows the exact spot. "I hope the rice is still there."

Hill 500 is an ideal lookout, one of the highest elevations on Lubang; unlike all the other peaks on the island, it is not overgrown. The protruding hump looks like a bald head sticking out, only a little knee-high grass grows here. It affords a view of the entire North and West of the island. Onoda and Shimada spend a very long time motionless in the shelter of the forest fringe. Something stirs there, below them, a sound. They stay rigidly still, with the barely possible patience of wild animals. To a panther in the open, it's perfectly natural. And Onoda is now an animal, a flecked animal. With his field glasses he sweeps the jungle in front of him, without the least expression. When he hands them to Shimada, it is in slow motion, where a simple gesture seems to take minutes—take weeks—as though they were an outgrowth of his hand that needed to be transplanted. Or is it just seconds, so deeply and intensely felt that they seemed to go on for months?

Flat fields to the North of the island, rice, coconut palms, a few tiny hamlets of five or six huts each, mounted on poles, roofed with palm leaves. Distant grumble of explosions. Up in the North, the seashore is covered with haze, with a distinct layer of darker haze hanging above it. Shimada spots fire on the airfield up there. He returns the field glasses. From now on, they only communicate in whispers. Onoda seems unmoved. "The Americans have bombed the runway," he whispers, "when they could have used it for their planes. It's a victory for us. Our first victory."

Emboldened, the two soldiers leave their hiding place, Onoda always on the very edge of the jungle, ready to give covering fire to Shimada, who is cautiously out in the open. He reaches a pile of dried palm fronds and starts pulling them away one at a time. Concealed underneath them is a number of metal bins, all empty. All except the last, which is full of rice. Wooden crates also hidden are bursting with ammunition, several thousand rifle bullets, machine-gun belts. Carefully the two soldiers recover their find. Onoda examines the rice, holds a few grains out in the light in the palm of his hand. No damp, no sign of mold. The trees around tremble gently. Onoda's hand trembles, too, not a genuine trembling but an involuntary quivering, like the skin of a horse trying to protect itself against flies. The few grains of rice fly off, apparently of their own volition. Then a pressure wave, and a split second later the thunder roll of a huge distant explosion. Onoda at once understands that this must have been the field hospital. The wounded men have blown themselves up, no question. Onoda and Shimada bow formally in the direction of the explosion, and hold the position for a long time.

After that, Onoda and Shimada are on their way, off into the decades that lie ahead of them. Often walking backward so that their traces are heading in the wrong direction. In this way, they encounter two more Japanese soldiers who are lying on the ground, rifles cocked. Straightaway Onoda and Shimada take cover. One of the other soldiers, expecting reinforcements, leaps up. Immediately he is struck by a volley of fire from the other side, and presumably killed. The second man makes the same mistake and embarks on a zigzag run toward Onoda, who opens fire in the direction of the unseen enemy. By some miracle, the man isn't hit. He drops down between Onoda and Shimada in a little hollow on the jungle's edge. Sounds of American voices, evidently retreating; the jungle is too dangerous for them. Onoda keeps the new arrival from checking on his comrade. A dead man would only be an impediment to them.

"Who are you?" asks Onoda.

"Private Kozuka."

"Who is the man over there?"

"Private Muranaka."

"I am in command here. If the Private is still alive, I will get him. Cover me." Onoda strips off his rucksack and pulls out his sword. Like a samurai in a deadly fury, he leaps up and races in a ritual attack straight toward the enemy, who has cleared his ambush. Onoda finds the man lying face-down and turns him over. He is dead.

Night. The men, three of them now, tend a small fire in a hollow among thick foliage. Onoda is preoccupied. "My sword attack was drama. I was playing a samurai in a film. An unforgivable lapse. The war is different now, heroic gestures have no place. Our tasks are to remain invisible, to deceive the enemy, to be ready to do seemingly dishonorable things while keeping safe in our hearts the warrior's honor."

The men have boiled some rice. They eat in silence. Then Kozuka tells them he was a member of the airfield ground crew. Originally there were seven of them. Four more had joined them, only to leave again hours later. They had

43

lacked a commander. "How was the ambush possible?" asks Onoda. Kozuka replies that no one expected the enemy to approach from the South. These must have come from the sea side of the island. They had felt perfectly safe, when suddenly they had come under fire. Only he and Muranaka had managed to get away to higher altitude.

"Who were the men killed? Do I know them?" Onoda asks.

"Ito, Suehiro, Kasai."

"I knew Kasai," says Onoda.

"Kasai was hit in the head. And then Osaki and just now Muranaka. We went to school together."

Silence comes over the men. Kozuka is so hungry that he scrapes the empty rice pot with his fingers. He had last eaten three days ago, before the airfield was taken. "What happened there?" Onoda asks; he had seen fire.

"American fighter planes made an unopposed attack and shot up the dummy planes on the runway," Kozuka reports.

"I put them there," says Onoda.

"So it was you who misled the enemy."

Onoda does not smile. "The Americans by themselves destroyed what might have been their next jumping-off point."

Kozuka is reluctant to carry on. "They didn't really destroy the runway."

"What do you mean?"

"They didn't drop any bombs. They didn't crater the surface."

"Oh?"

"They just strafed the dummy planes with their machine guns and set them on fire. The airstrip is mostly intact."

Onoda is silent. After a while he looks his new comrade in the eye. "I have lost my honor. First the pier at Tilik, which is still intact, and now the airstrip. From now on our watchword must be: attack the enemy, inflict losses on him, and withdraw."

Kozuka joins their tiny troop, which is now up to three men.

"We all in Lubang know that you would have sabotaged the pier at Tilik but for some senior officers. We can still carry out many tasks. The three of us will be able to oppose the enemy in many ways. They will never find us. The American patrols make too much noise, and they are wary of the jungle."

At night, once the men have set up a tent in the dense underbrush, and Kozuka is snoring fitfully, Onoda quietly goes up to Shimada, who is on watch. They briefly debate whether to keep the new arrival with them. They acknowledge that he is strong, and besides, he has no unit anymore, and no objective. Onoda would like him still to prove his worth. The following morning, he has disappeared. But when Onoda asks

Shimada quietly where he might be, they both hear Kozuka's voice. He is nearby, on watch, and so thickly camouflaged with leaves that he seems to be part of the jungle. Farther, he has found a source of fresh water only a few minutes below their position. One pan full, covered with a banana leaf, he has already boiled. When the members of the garrison were put to flight, they almost all suffered diarrhea from drinking out of streams. In all the years to come, the fight to remain healthy will be paramount. Except when they find pools of rainwater on large leaves, they will always boil their water.

Lubang, near Tilik

This is where the provisional field hospital once stood. Onoda and his two comrades cautiously explore the terrain. Tilik village, occupied by the invaders, is not far. Nothing is left to indicate what once, not long ago, was here. High up in a tree Onoda makes the surreal discovery of a boot, caught on its laces in a bough. It's a Japanese army boot. Leaving their cover, the soldiers approach and see something that makes their blood freeze. In front of them is a hollow crater, with a little water at the bottom of it. There is nothing left, no tent, no corpse, not even any body parts, everything has seemingly evaporated, dematerialized in the heat. The three men silently salute.

Onoda knows that they can survive only if they periodically break out into the open to provision themselves. The jungle will give them nothing. It is the acquisition of food that makes them vulnerable. Their thrusts must be quick and precise, and come after exhaustive observation of the scene. In the plain they are visible to the enemy; only at night or during torrential rain are they—possibly—safe. At nightfall they slink into a grove of palms and are surprised when a little girl walks by with her puppy dog. She is singing to herself and doesn't see them. The puppy stops to bark in Onoda's direction, but when the girl hurries on under the intensifying rain, it follows.

They pick up coconuts that are lying scattered on the ground, still in their stout green shells. At night in their refuge, the men try to crack the shells. Kozuka tries with his knife, Onoda stabs his with his bayonet. Unfortunately, this part of their education was neglected in military academy. It is Shimada who finds the solution. He sets the coconut down on a flat stone and strikes the tip of it with a big rock. The whole of the thick peel bulges outward. Then with a knife the dense web of green fibers easily permits itself to be detached from the nut.

"Of course," says Onoda. "The farm boy solves the problem."

"Not at all," counters Shimada, "that was just intelligence. On our farm we didn't grow coconuts."

It is perhaps their first moment of levity. The weight of the following decades will completely crush such moments, including this one. A sound. The men freeze. Kozuka touches his ear, motions with his head, down there somewhere. Cautiously, Onoda takes up his rifle. Is it the sound of a human being approaching? Now nothing stirs, just drips of rainwater from the trees.

"Cover me," Onoda indicates to Kozuka; he barely moves his lips, it is an inaudible whisper. He jumps up, charges off. A brief struggle in the tangle below the camp. A yell, a Japanese voice.

"I'm one of you. A friend. Japanese. Who are you?"

"First, who are you?" counters Onoda.

"Akatsu. Private Akatsu. I was part of the surviving airstrip garrison under Corporal Fujitsu."

"Why aren't you with them now?"

"And where is your gun?" asks Shimada. "We can only use men who are armed."

Akatsu apologizes. "We were in such a hurry that I left my rifle."

"A soldier doesn't exist without his rifle. It should be like a part of him," Onoda rebukes him. "I have a spare pistol in my rucksack, but very little ammunition."

Shimada seems to have more hostility toward the newcomer. "Why don't you return to your unit?"

"My unit was pulverized, the few men remaining are no longer on the island." He removes his spectacles. "I can't see in the dark. I'm practically night-blind." He polishes them on his neck cloth. "And when it rains, they fog up. Please let me go with you."

"You can stay until tomorrow morning. We'll decide what to do with you then," Onoda decrees.

Over the course of the long evening, Onoda and his two men learn Akatsu's story. His unit was almost without food, and what little they had soon disappeared. Akatsu was convinced that some of the men were thieving. They tried to deflect suspicion onto him, tried to get rid of him because he realized what was going on. He was twice sent away, but each time returned to the unit because he couldn't have survived on his own. Then a large part of the unit marched directly into a camp of Filipino troops who promptly opened fire on them. Five died, others surrendered, the remnant, more than forty strong, managed to reach a landing craft. He himself and two others, who were similarly blackballed by the unit, remained unhurt, but the two others abandoned him the following night. The enemy tried to induce the scattered survivors to surrender; over a loudspeaker they named a place, in Japanese, where Japanese soldiers could safely surrender, but Akatsu was unable to find it.

"Private Akatsu," Onoda asks him, "tell me which way is North."

Akatsu looks around cluelessly. No, he has no idea.

"Private Kozuka, which way is North," Onoda asks. Kozuka gestures cursorily with his head. Shimada nods in confirmation. Onoda takes his pistol out of his rucksack and hands it to Akatsu. "Do you know how to use one of these?"

Akatsu says sheepishly, "Yes. Not really. Vaguely."

"Then I'll have to teach you," says Onoda, and with that Akatsu has been provisionally inducted into their unit.

Following a cramped night in the tent that is too small for four men, Onoda decides to scrap it altogether; too much baggage, also it's an easy thing for the enemy to spot. From now on they never stop anywhere for more than a day at a time, from now on Onoda is in continual movement, sometimes even at night. Akatsu has trouble keeping up, he often drops off the pace. He apologizes to Onoda. "Lieutenant, I do my best, but I've never been in a jungle before."

"None of us has ever been in a jungle before," Onoda points out, but he has some sympathy with Akatsu, whose feet are bleeding because his boots don't fit properly.

"This is like a green hell," says Akatsu sadly.

"No, it's just a forest in the tropics," says Onoda.

Lubang, Looc Overlook

October 1945

At this point, the jungle falls steeply away. The Looc plain extends from here to the South coast. Coconut palms, rice paddies, one of them a little detached from the others, not part of the same irrigation system, the field of the one white-veiled woman. Haze. The little town of Looc is dimly visible on the broad sandy bay. There is no visible road communication to the North of the island, no ships in the bay, it's as though the Americans had never landed. Far in the distance, the islands of Golo and Ambil to the East, both of them militarily useless, just as Lubang was and now is again useless. It's only in theoretical invasion plans that Lubang has a strategic function as an island, with the added difficulty that it is peopled by ghosts. Onoda and his men look out.

A breath of wind blows through the jungle, shreds of spiders' webs are blown away, and with them the months, with nothing to hold them, no trembling twigs, no dripping rain. Nothing happened, only one or two breaths.

Months later: the same place, the same little troop, again silently surveying the plain below. Onoda and his three men have changed: they are better disguised; their hair is tangled; their clothing, equipment, and boots have all been smeared with clay for purposes of camouflage. They have become one with the jungle. Onoda orders Akatsu to fetch water from a little stream below their position, and while he is out of earshot, the other three discuss what is to be done with him. Shimada is undecided, Kozuka is in favor of ditching him. In their heart of hearts, they all wanted to be rid of him, he was a burden on them, the four of them were weaker than they would be if they were only three. But Onoda decides otherwise, even if Akatsu is a burden, he is still a soldier like the rest of them.

"Would you leave me behind if I were to fall ill?" he asks Kozuka. "Lieutenant!" Kozuka hastens to assure him he would take him on his back and carry him. The distant noise of a small plane approaching from the direction of Looc causes the men to freeze, and they melt back into the bush. Onoda tracks it with his field glasses. Once it reaches the steeply rising jungle near them, it seems to drop something that disperses on the wind, something like a bunch of confetti.

It takes Akatsu a long time to return from his task, so that the other three are wondering what could have befallen him. Did he lose his way? Did the plane alarm him? As night falls, there is a rustle in the underbrush, not before time. Akatsu identifies himself before they can start shooting at him. He apologizes for having spilled some of the water, but he had to take cover suddenly because of the plane. He had seen that what the plane had dropped must be leaflets. He had spotted one not far from where he was, caught up in the top of a tree. With difficulty he had climbed up it, got the leaflet, and been set upon by fire ants. And for a fact his hands are swollen and the lymph glands in his armpits are up. He felt feverish, but he had managed to find his way back because he remembered that Looc was to the South, and so he knew which way was North, and their current hideout. With painful fingers he tries to pull the folded leaflet out of his breast pocket, but they are so swollen that Onoda has to help him. The paper is cheap, the text on it is printed in Japanese.

The men pore over the text, which is signed by General Yamashita, Fourteenth Army, and dated August 15. The war is over, it says.

"But it's October now," says Kozuka blandly, "and it doesn't even say who won." And there's another thing as well, something that will pull together reasoned doubts into a consistent conclusion: there are mistakes in some of the Japanese characters. Onoda is the first to notice. All Japanese soldiers are to emerge from the jungle into "open scenery" and surrender their weapons to the Philippine Army. It sounds like a bad translation, from someone who doesn't really know the Japanese language. And a further mistake: "You will be 'conveyanced' home." The only possible conclusion is that this leaflet is a forgery, presumably the work of American agents. A misprint is out of the question, even if the Japanese character for *return, convey* resembles the one for *conveyance*. They must ask themselves why the enemy air force is still after them, and why Filipino troops were only recently ambushing and killing Japanese troops, as the example of Akatsu proved. Nevertheless, Akatsu remains doubtful; what if the war really is over? But Onoda is unshakably convinced that all this is just a trick to lure them out of their jungle fastness.

"But what if the war really is lost?" Akatsu pipes up again. But that only reinforces Onoda in his certainty that the Japanese forces will one day gloriously return and retake Lubang. The island was of great strategic importance, and from here the Japanese forces would swarm out to retake the whole Pacific. Their orders were orders.

There is a long pause. Shimada gnaws at a creeper. Kozuka whittles away at a piece of wood. Onoda looks around. "Does anyone here want to surrender?" He fixes on Akatsu. "Private Akatsu, you are free to go if you want; I'm not forcing you to do anything."

What did the others think? Akatsu wants to know. "Lieutenant, if you go on fighting, I will stay with you."

"And you, Private Kozuka?"

"Stay."

Onoda looks at Akatsu again. "Well, Private?"

"I'm staying too. Where would I go by myself?"

A further leaflet confirms Onoda's by now almost religious belief in the incompetence of the enemy and his forgeries. It mentions the prefecture of Wakayama, Onoda's home, as though to make him homesick. But the clinching evidence is the name of his battalion. This name was altered just a matter of weeks before the Japanese strategic withdrawal, for what reason Onoda cannot say, but the new name sounded braver, and more victorious: "The Cradle of Storms. We will pass over the enemy like a typhoon and blow him away."

At this point, incidentally, a new phenomenon begins, a sort of constant, unobtrusive companionship, a natural dream sibling equipped with all the unquestioning certainty of dreams: a shapeless time of noctambulism, even though things carry on as before, immediate, palpable, ghastly, undeniable in their imperiousness—the jungle; the swamp; the leeches; the mosquitoes; the screams of the birds; thirst; the bumpy, itching skin. The dream has its own time frame, it races forward and back, it sticks, stops dead, holds its breath, jumps ahead like a frightened deer. A night bird shrieks and a year passes. A fat drop of water on the waxy leaf of a banana plant glistens briefly in the sun and another year is gone. A column of millions and millions of ants arrives overnight and marches through the trees with no beginning or end; the column marches for days and days and then one day is mysteriously and suddenly gone, and that is another year. Then one single watch under withering enemy fire, and the night seems to go on forever and ever. Only the abrupt flares of tracer bullets while day refuses to break, even though you look at your watch and see the hands moving and see the whole of the night sky wheeling around the North Star. Day will not and will not and will not arrive. Time outside their lives seems to have the quality of a spasm, even though it can't shake the imperturbable universe. Onoda's war is of no meaning for the cosmos, for history, for the course of the war. Onoda's war is formed from the union of an imaginary nothing and a dream, but Onoda's war, sired by nothing, is nevertheless overwhelming, an event extorted from eternity.

LUBANG, JUNGLE, AGCAWAYAN RIVER

U p in the mountains with their dense growth of jungle, the river is just a clear stream cascading down over flat rocks; it's not until it reaches the plains between the villages of Agcawayan and Ten House that it becomes sluggish, swampy, and wide. Onoda and his men are washing their clothes, but never all of them, because they must always be prepared for any eventuality. One man, Kozuka, is deputed to keep watch. Onoda's uniform jacket is in bad shape. One of the breast pockets is almost torn off. It's less the brush, the thorns, the stress of continual movement that destroys the clothes; more simply it's the rot in the jungle, the humidity that erodes all materials.

Not far from Ten House, a footbridge has been thrown across the swamp. There Kozuka encounters a piece of chewing gum stuck to the underside of one of the bamboo poles used as bridge rails. The chewing gum is used. The question is: Has a local stuck the piece of gum there, or was it a GI? Onoda and his men know that Filipino villagers don't chew gum—that would be highly improbable. But they have observed that this vice is common among American soldiers. So are there American soldiers still stationed on Lubang? How long has the piece of gum been there? Days? Months? How does gum behave when exposed to tropical conditions? On closer inspection, and with a little imagination, it is possible to see the imprint of a molar, and beside it that of another tooth, slightly deformed. Everything suggests a wisdom tooth, but do Americans have wisdom teeth? Are they at all like other men? Are their voices not louder than those of the normal run of human beings? And is it perhaps conceivable that the gum was deliberately placed there, to mislead the guerrilla fighters? What to do? Akatsu is inclined to try chewing it to gain a sense of what this gum is like. What does it feel like, to be chewing gum? What do Americans feel—if, that is, they are even capable of feeling? Onoda orders the gum to be left exactly where they found it.

Some months later, he comes upon the gum again, but he is absolutely certain that it's been moved by a hand's breadth, also that it looks flatter. There is a long discussion of the matter, but Onoda can exactly remember how far from the upright the gum was stuck to the underside of the rail. Which can only mean one thing: the gum has been chewed and replaced. Kozuka takes Onoda aside and confides a suspicion he has. Could it be that in some unobserved moment Akatsu has tested the chewing gum? And could it be that the chewing gum was poisoned or contained some drug that weakens body and spirit? Or perhaps it was Shimada who secretly tasted the chewing gum, and is now deflecting suspicion upon Akatsu to be rid of him? Under interrogation, Akatsu denies ever having touched the chewing gum. Shimada, similarly questioned, is offended for several days and becomes withdrawn. For some time, the common purpose of the men is disrupted because Onoda fails to ask Kozuka the same question—as though of all of them Kozuka were the only one to be above suspicion.

Back now—back to Onoda's men, now cautiously approaching Ten House. The few huts are all set on poles. Evening quiet prevails, with the murmur of voices. Hens scratch around in the sand unafraid, right in front of Onoda. A dog appears from somewhere, and half-heartedly barks at the intruders from a safe distance. Onoda jumps up and fires a shot into one of the palm frond roofs, makes it spurt up. The hens scatter. Two or three more shots in rapid succession. Cries from the villagers.

"Hold your fire!" calls Onoda. "Let them flee." When they have all disappeared in a cloud of dust in the direction of Tilik, Onoda's men go through the huts. Onoda will not permit looting. Kozuka is on the point of stashing a tin can full of sugar in his rucksack when Onoda rebukes him: they were soldiers, not thieves. The only things the troop picks up are a screwdriver, some wire, a sewing needle, matches, and some basic provisions, for instance rice. Shimada takes a couple of pieces off a washing line: a towel, some cloth with which they could patch perhaps their uniforms. Akatsu finds a large bolo knife. Suddenly the sound of a truck alarms him. Before the enemy is even in sight, he is already firing away. Akatsu fires back blindly; Shimada, too, is shooting in the direction of the unseen foe.

"Cease-fire!" calls Onoda.

But Shimada carries on. "They're shooting at us!"

Onoda grabs him by the arm. "They are afraid. They can't even see us. They are just making noise."

A bullet rips through a tree branch over Shimada. A Filipino country policeman takes cover behind a loaded cart. Onoda fires at him. He and his men retreat rapidly. Once back in the jungle, Onoda's small force hastens forward. Akatsu falls behind. When Kozuka offers to take his rucksack, Onoda forbids it. Every man must carry his own load. He leaves the clay path and plunges into the steeply rising jungle.

Lubang, Jungle, Snake Mountain

December 1945

The men have spread out their loot on a piece of burlap, everything is important for their survival. A feeling of relief in the provisional campsite. Evening darkens over the jungle. Their matches, unfortunately, have gotten damp. Shimada tells the others they are no longer usable. Even if they were dried out in the sun, they would no longer strike. How did he know such a thing? wonders Kozuka. He grew up on a farm, Shimada reminds him.

At nightfall, Onoda defines the new sleeping arrangements. He crawls off under a bush, the terrain is sloping.

"You should find a place that is on a slope. If the enemy approaches, you will see him without having to get up. Keep your rifles by your side at all times. Cover yourselves with a piece of camouflaged burlap, and your legs placed on a rucksack. That way, you won't slide downhill in your sleep. The rucksack is to be kept packed and ready. You must be prepared to vanish in a matter of seconds. Rubbish and excrement are to be buried at once, and carefully covered over with leaves and twigs. No one is ever to see the least trace of where we made camp. No one is to know where we spent the night, or by what route we marched." The men say nothing, they have understood. And then Onoda explains how he sees their respective roles.

"I am not your commander. You have not been allocated to me by High Command. I am your leader."

The following morning, the men set about repairing their clothes and equipment. Kozuka, who has disassembled his rifle, remarks that all parts of it are covered with a fine layer of rust, the jungle damp has gotten in everywhere. Onoda carefully draws his sword from its sheath, it, too, shows signs of rust. There are coconuts everywhere, but how do you make palm oil? No one knows, not even the farm boy Shimada. An attempt to crush some white coconut flesh between two rocks gets nowhere. Then Kozuka remembers a cook who once worked in Europe, in an Italian restaurant. He later lived next to his family's cobbler shop. Kozuka remembers the cook talking about the label on Italian olive oil: extra virgin. "What did that have to do with coconuts?" Onoda asks. Kozuka remembers his conversation with the cook: extra virgin oil was expensive because the olives were not heated. So olive oil can otherwise be made using heat. It will take weeks more before the soldiers succeed in distilling palm oil. They begin by requisitioning a large cooking pot from a village; then they grind up the flesh of coconuts and mix it with water and heat the rough mash over an unusually large flame. Because the smoke would be easily visible, they wait for a day; the jungle is misty. First, a thick froth is precipitated, and after that subsides, a layer of oil, which can be carefully scooped up. Thenceforth, Onoda is able to keep his firearm and his family heirloom in good condition for almost thirty years. Bullets, which are also perishable, are kept upright in oil, sealed in stolen mason jars, and buried in the jungle, all in all two thousand four hundred rifle rounds, several hundred pistol rounds, and several hundred large-caliber rounds for machine guns. Onoda insists that they not be thrown away, before long they will prove their use in making fires. Because how do you light a fire without a supply of dry matches? They make many vain attempts to turn a stick in their hands over a piece of dry wood to make enough friction to create a flame. This was the method Onoda learned in his course for specialist warfare, but here everything is too damp for it to work.

Only a few months later, from secretly observing a few Filipino woodcutters through their field glasses, do they pick up the method the islanders use to make fire out of doors. They split an arm-thick piece of bamboo in two lengthwise, and make one of them fast to the ground, like a rail. The other one is carefully cut open, a little cut that barely penetrates the bamboo. Two men on their knees, facing each other, take the free half of bamboo, with the incision, and rub it quickly back and forth over the rail. The pressure and friction produce so much heat that a small pile of bamboo shavings eventually begins to glow. Whenever there is rain or the air is particularly damp, Onoda likes to add a little powder from the machine-gun ammunition, which otherwise would have had no use. After brief, violent rubbing, a small flame shoots out.

In the course of one retreat, they lose Akatsu, who once again has fallen behind. Kozuka, sent out as a search party, is unable to find him. A torrential rain begins to fall. The feet of the men, who have sought shelter under a large tree, are covered in mud, mosquitoes, and leeches. Even large leaves, held over their heads, cannot prevent the rain from getting everywhere. The monstrous clatter of water enjoins everything to silence, man and nature alike.

Lubang, Hill 500 Summit

Because Akatsu is still gone after two days, Onoda, Shimada, and Kozuka rebury the stock of munitions in a new place so that, in the event that Akatsu has fallen into enemy hands, he cannot betray the hiding place. The jungle around the bare knob of 500 is more suitable anyway because from there you can take in the treeless summit. Only with a gigantic numerical advantage would the enemy risk coming up here. Onoda oils his sword once more, wrapping handle and sheath in rattan, and lowering it vertically into a hollow tree. He carefully seals up the place with earth and moss.

Akatsu turns up unexpectedly on the middle of the jungle path that leads up to the summit. He is vastly relieved to have found his unit again, even if he did leave distinct tracks on the path. He says he lost contact when a strap on his rucksack tore. He shows them how he has tried to repair it with a liana. He had then lost his way, and walked almost as far as Tilik before realizing his mistake. There was nobody there on Snake, and he had just wandered around randomly. In another five years, in early 1950, Akatsu will leave the unit for the last time, and surrender to Filipino troops.

From away in the distance, they hear the patter of gunfire, and mortar explosions. Yes, the enemy has found Akatsu's trail, but Onoda keeps a clear head. Mortars are something you should only use when you know the enemy's exact position; this here is just the production of noise, a sign of fear, something to indicate to the local populace that the Japanese guerrillas are bravely being gone after. Greater danger would come from silence. Lubang is so small that it is possible to lay several traps at once, whole webs of them even. In the thirty years, just under, of his solitary war, Onoda will survive one hundred eleven ambushes.

Three months after Akatsu's surrender, Onoda and his now two men look on as a truck laden with great wooden crates is driven up Six Hundred Mountain, which affords a view of the village of Gontin and the Bay of One House Village.

The crates turn out to be loudspeakers. Fragments of a voice are blown up to them, difficult to make out, but recognizably Japanese. After listening hard, the men agree that it is Akatsu's voice, assuring them that Akatsu was being treated with respect. Not impossible that a voice imitator was used, though. Onoda assumes Akatsu has been tortured, to make him speak. The voice repeats, it is evidently a tape, assuring them that the Filipinos would let Akatsu go home, but Onoda becomes more and more certain that this is all an enemy ruse to get him to give up. As smoke is blown away on the wind, so the breeze disperses the voice. And it soon becomes apparent that the campaign is to be resumed. Activity in the air and naval maneuvers point to the opening of a new front somewhere to the West. But that was already the war after, for America.

Rice Paddy, Northern Plain of Lubang

Early 1946

The rice fields here stretch almost to the edge of the jungle. A couple of water buffalo are wallowing in a pond, submerged up to their backs in the muddy water. Every so often one waggles its ears. On a field track is another, solitary, buffalo harnessed to a two-wheeled cart, his head so low he looks to be asleep on his feet. A small group of rice farmers, dressed in wide-brimmed straw hats, shirts, and loincloths, is bending over and toiling away, calf deep in water. Each time one moves his feet there's a smacking sound, otherwise complete silence; they do their work in silence, planting the new rice shoots in the mud under the water. Other than a sense of the day coming to an end, there is no indication of the time. It's as though it were forbidden—there's not even a real sense of present because each performed action is already in the past, and each ensuing one is future. All here are outside history, which in its taciturnity will not allow present. The rice is planted, harvested, planted again. Kingdoms fall into decay. Stillness. In the silence of eternities, shots ring out. The peasants flee.

From the jungle perimeter Onoda and his two men come charging out into the open. Each one knows what he must do. Onoda fires one more shot in the direction of the fleeing peasants, Kozuka kills the buffalo harnessed to the cart with a peremptory shot in the head, Shimada with brisk movements sets about severing the hind legs of the dead beast. They are old hands at this, having done it all many times before. Kozuka cuts long strips of meat along the backbone. There is no attack to be feared from the distant village. The other water buffalo, standing in the mire, bored, show no emotion. Then, laden with their heavy bounty, the men withdraw. In addition to the strips of meat over his rucksack, Onoda is carrying a buffalo leg in his arms, as though bringing a wounded companion to safety. The men know that in the approaching darkness not even a well-armed troop of the enemy will dare follow them into the jungle.

"Fog is our best friend," observes Onoda, while continuing to rake the smoking fire with a stick. The whole jungle is fogbound, a light drizzle is falling. Only in conditions like this can the men keep the smoke and hence their whereabouts secret. Shimada keeps putting pieces of bark into the flames, which lighten the color of the smoke to match the white fog. On a jury-rigged spit, strips of meat are hanging to smoke. In the hot, damp climate untreated meat spoils inside two days. There is a time for meat, a time for coconuts, a time for rice. Onoda attacks the rice harvests—usually taking two sacks of rice, no more. He doesn't want to have too many soldiers dispatched to find him, he would like to keep the island free of Philippine forces, if possible. On its eventual return, the Imperial Army should not have to encounter too many enemy troops. When on one occasion he penetrates the center of Tilik, there is a direct exchange of fire. There are wounded on the Filipino side, and Shimada is hit in the leg, which will bother him for a long time to come. At bottlenecks where Onoda can be counted on to pass through often, there are repeated ambushes, with brief firefights. Onoda's caution is the caution of a wild animal. The steep overgrown slopes are relatively safe, but there is now not one watering place on Lubang that is not without some risk. But there are also moments when Onoda will suddenly come bursting out of the brush, and fire a shot over the heads of the terrified locals, merely to show them that he is still there, still occupying the island of Lubang. He has become a legend. For the locals he is the spirit of the jungle, only to be talked of in whispers. For the Philippine Army, which seems incapable of catching him, he is a permanent reminder of their incapacity, though at the same time the troops speak of him with the degree of affection one might have for a mascot. Two soldiers who purposely aim their guns way over his head during a skirmish are disciplined. But there are dead among the Philippine forces as well, and among the natives. Onoda never spoke about it in detail, nor are there any reliable figures from the Philippine authorities. And in Japan, meanwhile, the newspapers keep his solitary war continually before the attention of their readership, emphasizing the myth of the brave solitary soldier, at the same time keeping alive a painful reminder of Japan's defeat in the World War.

LUBANG

RAINY SEASON, 1954

Every day, Onoda and his two men are on the move. Never do they leave the least trace of themselves. Only in the three months of the rainy season do they have any sense of security. Troops will hardly be dispatched during the typhoon's apocalypse, and for the duration of that period, Onoda builds a solid shelter of saplings with a raised floor. The structure is always put up somewhere in the thickest and steepest part of the jungle, and the roof of woven palm fronds is never closed, so that the part facing the valley is left half open, leaving a view of possible encroaching enemies.

A drainage ditch protects the hut from flooding from above, and there is an outside toilet tucked away from the main building. Supplies of rice, green cooking bananas, and smoked meat are kept secure in a special niche. This period is particularly appreciated by the three of them as a time of relative tranquility. They repair their equipment, sleep undisturbed, and the days go by without strain. Only once, after years like this, does the rainy season hold off for three weeks or more, and a hostile force comes dangerously close to their hiding place without discovering it. Then the rain recommences and goes on for weeks longer than usual. In the uncertainty of the hours and days, routines create a frail sense of security. The men only ever have disagreements when they feel threatened. Onoda intelligently does nothing to prevent these, and their mutual rage eventually blows over.

The rainy season is also the time for storytelling. Kozuka, of course, clams up, his companions learn hardly anything about him, his family, their small shoemaking business, his young wife who was pregnant when his call-up came. He is forever wondering whether the baby is a boy or girl, and it's more than he can do to understand that he now has a ten-year-old of some description. Shimada is more open, he likes to laugh, talks endlessly about his home on the farm and about tools and machines. But both are insatiable when it comes to Onoda and his stories of his family and his childhood. Even after years spent together, these stories are inexhaustible because of the way Onoda keeps stumbling upon details he has never mentioned. All his comrades know of him is that, following his older brother to China, he made a great deal of money as a very young man in a trading post in Hankow, but it is only after twenty years that he includes the fact—as though it were something to be mortally ashamed of—that at the age of nineteen he was the owner of a Studebaker, a make of American car. The young Onoda was the first person in China to drive a Studebaker.

Shimada's curiosity is piqued. "Did the girls like the car?"

Onoda thinks about it. "They liked the car better than they liked me." But then he adds quietly that one of the girls must have liked him quite a lot, so much in fact that when he took up with someone else, she tried to kill herself. He had dealt frivolously with women and their emotions; from the point of view of today, his behavior was unprincipled. How had he then become the conscientious soldier who at any moment, night and day, rain and shine, under attack and whilst being hunted, stood unshakably to his duty? Kozuka asks. Onoda needs to think about it. It had probably begun with his return to Japan, and particularly when he became interested in martial arts. The turning point likely came with his training in kendo, or stick fighting. With that, he had come to understand something of the Japanese spirit, and his eyes were finally fully opened when he joined the army. But kendo had shown him that all forms of physical combat can be reduced to an essence, two men fighting with two sticks.

Again and again, the men come to this point in their conversations. What should war look like? How could it be simplified? In their practice of it, with no recourse to army, artillery, navy, or bomber planes? But then what about their own firearms, the standard-issue army rifles they use? From his study of guerrilla warfare, Onoda knows there was a time once when firearms, though already in widespread use, were given up almost overnight. It is his favorite subject, endlessly fascinating to him. Early in the seventeenth century, without any formal decision having been made, the samurai had given up their firearms. From that time on, all combat was man-to-man, with swords or lances, occasionally bows and arrows. What marked the beginning of this was a great battle in 1603 in which only twenty-six fighters still used firearms. Shimada objects that firearms were used after all, but Onoda points out that in a great battle ten years previous, some hundred and eighty thousand men fought on one side; there was documented proof of this. Roughly one-third of this army had carried firearms, making some sixty thousand men. No one could say with the same precision what the figures for the other side were, but it was safe to say that a hundred thousand muskets were used, plus cannon and falconets. Therefore, a mere twenty-six muskets a decade later was close to the complete absence of firearms. What had happened then, Shimada wants to know. They made a comeback, says Onoda. How long people got by without them was uncertain. By and by they had come back into use.

"Sometimes," says Onoda, "it feels to me that there is something about these weapons that takes them out of human control. Do they have a life of their own, as soon as they're devised? And doesn't war seem to have a life of its own too? Does war dream of war?" And then, after a long time mulling over such thoughts, Onoda says something he rarely says, as though the idea were a piece of metal brought to white heat in the fire: "Is it possible that I am dreaming this war? Could it be that I'm wounded in some hospital and will finally come out of a coma years later, and someone will tell me it was all a dream? Is the jungle, the rain—everything here—a dream? Is Lubang nothing but a fantasy that exists only on old mariners' charts, along with sea monsters and humans with the heads of dragons and dogs?"

And so the days go by. The rain pounds on their shelter. Water comes down the mountain swilling leaves and soil and torn-off twigs with it. When the rain lets up, the men check their ammunition that has been stored upright in oil-filled mason jars that were intended for canning fruit and making jam; they work on their boots and their uniforms, which are barely a memory of uniforms. The men cook and eat and sleep and sleep and eat and cook throughout the shapeless gray days of water streaming from the clouds and fogs boiling up in nature's sublime indifference. Every year, Onoda produces his family sword from its hiding place, and carefully cleans and oils it. Even if he was living in fever dreams, the sword remains his most palpable reference point for something that cannot be invented; an anchor dropped in a distant reality.

But then reality resumes sway. Kozuka is sick, there is blood in his urine, and Shimada brews him a tea made from jungle plants. His condition remains unaffected. Kozuka suddenly hates everything, the jungle, the rain, the war, the tea, which he goes on drinking just in case. Ammunition seems to be real, too, not the actual bullets themselves but their numbers, even though numbers are not palpable. Whenever he cleans the bullets and moves them on into a fresh palm oil bath, Onoda holds a census. He makes use of little sticks that he lays out on the ground and moves according to a system of his own invention, a sort of private abacus, which also does duty as a calendar. There are two thousand six hundred rifle bullets left; they have an average annual consumption of forty. But despite all his caution, he has noticed some signs of oxidation, and, of late, some bullets have refused to fire. In theory, the bullets ought to be good for another sixty years of warfare, but Onoda emphasizes economy in their use. What if the foe were to launch a sudden all-out attack? What if one of their caches were to be discovered? How old would he, Onoda, be at the time he used his last bullet?

LUBANG, JUNGLE PERIPHERY

1954

The rainy season is over. The jungle is steaming. Millions of birds break out in jubilation. The men survey the terrain. Onoda scans the edge of the forest, where it goes over into open country. His field glasses have suffered over the years, the damp has gotten into them, and a milky fungus has spread over the lenses. But even with the naked eye he can see that the cattle are close to the edge of the jungle, where a strip of fresh grass has been let stand. It is only on the far side of that that the rice paddies begin. Shimada is happy that for once their prey has come to them, it means the meat won't have to be lugged quite so far.

There is one cow grazing less than ten yards from the jungle periphery. The soldiers, well hidden, keep still. Without moving, they survey the surroundings. There is nothing out of the ordinary. Shimada, finally, impatient, leaves the shelter of the dense foliage and approaches the cow, his rifle leveled at her head. Then all hell breaks loose. Fire from two sides; a carefully planned ambush. Shreds of twigs fly up from the bushes where the bullets are coming from. Shimada spins around to return fire, but at that very moment he is struck in the head. He drops like a felled tree trunk. Onoda and Kozuka fire away wildly. In a panic a couple of Filipino soldiers take to their heels. One of them is hit by Onoda, and dragged back into cover by his comrades. Onoda's rifle jams, and he is unable to shoot. But the enemy is already withdrawing. After a brief moment's thought, under covering fire from Kozuka, Onoda rushes up to Shimada, but a glance is enough to tell him he's past help, he's dead. Enraged, Onoda blindly fires into the thick jungle the enemy has withdrawn into.

Lubang, West Coast

1971

Twenty-six years now after the end of the war. Another dawn breaks over the island. The sun detaches itself from the horizon in a flare of red and orange. Striations of rain hang over the lowlands. Strange insects go crawling up the jungle lianas, hard to know what they're about. Onoda observes B-52 bombers high in the sky, leaving their fourfold vapor trails. Onoda is now past fifty, and more resigned, more stoical than ever. The coast here is black volcanic rock, interspersed with small sandy beaches. Behind it the mountains rise steeply, covered in jungle. The actual coast is dangerous, exposed to view from far and wide. Onoda is lying on his back, Kozuka is mounting guard. Onoda hands him the field glasses. Over one eye, the lenses are less comprehensively overgrown with fungus.

Onoda is convinced that this is a new generation of bombers, which they have been observing now since 1966 or so. The squadrons of them are getting larger all the time. "Americans?" inquires Kozuka.

Onoda is in no doubt about it, even though he can't see the blazons from so far below. "From Clark Air Base?" speculates Kozuka, but Onoda is doubtful. "It's not possible for such heavy planes to rise so steeply over such a short distance. Presumably these are from Guam." That would also be the logical explanation for the shift of the theater of war toward Southeast Asia or India. What made him think of India?

"India," explains Onoda, "has freed itself from the British, and Siberia has split away from Russia. They have now joined Japan, to form a powerful triple alliance against America." Kozuka is restless. They had spent far too long here exposed to view. Onoda orders a rapid retreat up into the steep jungled slopes.

A resting place in the thick of the jungle. Birdsong, furious mosquitoes. The two men are standing, pressed close together. Onoda, technically gifted, has long concluded that this new generation of aircraft no longer uses propellers. Given the altitude they fly at, they must be able to fly much faster than any propeller rotation could achieve.

"Why?" asks Kozuka.

"Because the air gets so thin up there that a plane can stay airborne only if it flies extremely rapidly." Onoda holds out a bottle horizontally to demonstrate the principle: there must be a closed chamber in which the fuel is burned almost explosively, with an opening at the back. The released energy from the explosion forces the chamber forward, just as a garden hose would recoil from its opening if one didn't hold on to it.

"But how is it that the explosion or succession of explosions doesn't destroy the chamber and the plane?" asks Kozuka.

"A car does the same thing—thousands of explosions per minute in the interior of the engine without destroying it," Onoda quells him. It was his hope that one of these planes might crash-land on Lubang, and give him an opportunity to inspect one of these jet engines.

LUBANG, HILL 500

1971

Onoda and Kozuka are on the move. Each step they take is circumspect and slow. They keep within the cover of the jungle until they reach the bald summit of Hill 500. Something is different here. Then they see it, a small card table has been set up, with a thick roll of paper on it wrapped in plastic. A sign has been placed in the grass. It reads "News from Japan" in Japanese characters. Onoda and Kozuka keep their eyes on it until it gets dark, not until the following morning do they dare leave the security of their concealment. Onoda carefully nudges the roll this way and that with the muzzle of his rifle, before taking it in his hand. A newspaper, no doubt about it, freshly printed. It has been here two days at the most; someone must have been up here immediately before them. Hurriedly the two soldiers withdraw into the shelter of the jungle.

Not until they get to the Looc Overlook, from where it is possible to see enemy movements a long way off, do they throw themselves upon their find, pore over the newspaper centimeter by centimeter. Onoda turns it over, sees advertisements for electrical kitchen equipment, for cars, for lipstick. He turns back to the front-page headline: Australia and New Zealand are ending their involvement in the war. A further column: the calamitous South Vietnamese offensive in Laos. Below it a photograph, with soldiers desperately clinging on to an American helicopter flying out the wounded.

Why would America be supporting Vietnam? Onoda wonders. Has the theater of war moved farther West, as he concluded years ago, or has Laos now joined India, China, and Siberia in the new anti-American alliance? Kozuka thinks it's possible. Onoda, though, remains doubtful, and wonders whether the newspaper isn't a forgery from the American secret service. Why didn't he think of that right away? But Kozuka points to the small ads, which look pretty genuine to him. Onoda turns over the pages again and again, and finally determines that the enemy has gained access to a genuine newspaper, and merely tampered with certain pages. Some important things, Kozuka observes, were completely passed over, such as Japan's role in this war. And the many columns of advertisements are a better alternative than blacking out whole pages. "Aside from the front page," Onoda calculates, "almost half the print surface consists of advertisements. But newspapers have never assigned more than two or three percent of their space for advertising. No one will ever buy all this stuff, that's completely impossible. They've censored the actual news, and replaced it with advertising."

Kozuka's attention is once more drawn to the front page, which is dated March 19, 1971. This is final, conclusive evidence of falsification for Onoda: the edition is predated. "Today is March 15; the numbskulls don't even know how to count properly."

"But what if—" Kozuka objects.

Onoda looks at him sharply. "What if what?"

"What if our calendar wasn't quite right," says Kozuka, "just supposing."

"It is," Onoda assures him, "I worked in all the leap years, I've observed the moons—"

"The moon can play tricks," says Kozuka.

Onoda reflects. "Correct. The lunar phases are not helpful in making a calendar, and when we were on the run, I wasn't always able to keep track of the days. Also, because we're so close to the equator here, it's difficult to measure the summer and winter solstices accurately. But even with all that, I still know how to count."

"I apologize, Lieutenant," says Kozuka.

Darkness has fallen. The two men continue to stare at every line, every photograph, every ad. A small fire provides sufficient light, they hold the newspaper right up to their faces, their heads seem to glow from the fire. Something is bothering Onoda. He listens. Nothing. Then he freezes, reaches for his rifle.

"Something's up," he whispers.

Kozuka hunches down, strains his ears. But then Onoda discovers something that might appear to be the most natural thing in the world, but to him it is an absolute sensation.

"Look, there's Looc. They've got electricity." And indeed, the little town is lit up by some neon tubes, an incredible event. The two soldiers haven't seen electricity for maybe five years, the last time was in Lubang township, from a distance. Onoda assumes they are in for some harder times now, especially at night, when the enemy can switch on great searchlights and look for them. Kozuka just wants to appreciate the change.

The following day, Onoda makes another discovery through his fogged field glasses. Six farmers are laboring out in the open, but they are accompanied by two men in civvies who are carrying rifles. Not soldiers, clearly, but sentries, guarding them while they work. How to react? Onoda decides on an attack. It's been too long since they've shown who's boss.

Lubang, the Lowlands near Looc

1971

Onoda and Kozuka are flattening themselves through long grass, creeping forward in the manner of a lioness approaching her prey. A few palms, some papayas in amongst them. The peasants are laughing as they work.

"Where are the two sentries?" whispers Onoda.

Kozuka spots them. "Left-hand side, under the canvas sunroof, you can just see them."

Onoda strains his ears. "I can hear music."

"A radio? How can a radio be playing out here in the open?" Kozuka whispers. Onoda decides to attack. He jumps out, opens fire. The peasants scream, flee in all directions. One of the sentries tries to fire a shot, but evidently his gun isn't even loaded. The other peppers away in the general direction of

Onoda, but only hits pebbles on the ground that go skittering up, though one bullet ricochets and hits Onoda in the foot. An hour later, he will realize he has bled into his boot. The field has been vacated by its defenders. Kozuka grabs a sack of rice, a machete, a few papayas. Onoda takes the little shortwave radio that is still playing music from the local station. The voice of a Tagalog-speaking DJ is spreading mindless merriment. The speaker is fairly weak, and at first Onoda can't find the off button. He doesn't want to give away their position as they retreat.

"Desde la Capital del Tango, desde Buenos Aires," Onoda hears from the loudspeaker when he finally gets a chance to look for a station in the security of a hiding place under a rock promontory. How can it be possible to pick up Buenos Aires, half a world away? wonders Kozuka. For himself, Onoda is amused at what Kozuka was taught at school. These were shortwave signals that are shot up to the stratosphere and then bounced around to various parts of the world. Because the volume is so low and drags, Onoda takes the thing apart, and concludes the batteries are almost dead. But something else surprises him. This radio has no tubes, so there must have been some extraordinary advance. He wipes the batteries and puts them back in. A lot of static, fragments of various languages, and then suddenly, for under a minute, the climax of a Beethoven piano sonata. Then a Japanese station. Because the volume is so feeble, and the reception comes and goes, both men press their ears to the little loudspeaker, and their heads lie together. A horse race is being broadcast.

"And now," the radio speaker announces, "the second event of the evening, the Kyoto Grand. The favorite is Cherry Blossom, the mare . . ."

"Six furlongs, unbelievable, I can hardly remember what a horse looks like," whispers Kozuka.

"And proof," gloats Onoda, "that Japan is doing extremely well in the war. Do you think they'd be staging horse races otherwise?"

The reception keeps cutting out, but it is undoubtedly a race meet. "And now Pride of Hokkaido . . . takes the lead, the field is spread out on the final straight . . ."

Because the batteries are so weak, Onoda warms them in his armpits.

"Here is the lineup for race number four: Plumed Arrow, Bird of Prey, White Shadow, the previous winner of the Tokyo Open, prancing nervously . . ."

"We could bet on the winner," suggests Kozuka.

"I don't think so, I don't know the first thing about these racehorses of yours," Onoda objects. Kozuka nods.

But then Onoda has a change of heart. "Very well, I bet on White Shadow, he sounds like a winner."

Kozuka plumps for Bird of Prey. But the loudspeaker has a surprise in store for them.

"Oh, no, no, no, NO," goes the commentator's voice. "White Shadow has broken out of the starting box and has thrown his rider. White Shadow with empty saddle, crosses the track and makes for the car park. Stable lads are in pursuit, but how will they find the stallion among twenty thousand parked cars? Now the race must begin without him."

"Twenty thousand, incredible," mutters Kozuka.

"Once when I was on the track," Onoda recalls, "there were a lot of buses and maybe two hundred cars. Not more."

Then, smiling, he makes a suggestion: "If you correctly pick the winner, that would speak to your superior intelligence, and you could be my boss for one day."

Several times both men draw blanks, but then, in one race that is practically inaudible, Kozuka bets on Samurai Number One. The name is hardly mentioned, but suddenly the breathless commentator goes: "Shinjuku has the lead, but is flagging badly. Out of nowhere, Samurai Number One surges forward. He has come right up from the back, now he's in the lead, it's neck and neck. Samurai Number One is the winner by a short head."

Onoda congratulates Kozuka on his winning instinct. The next day Kozuka is the leader, but he has no idea what to do with his promotion. Over the decades, his subordinate role has so come to define him that he is hardly in a position to issue a simple command. But the men laugh about it, and it becomes a rather jolly day of minor mishaps. Because the batteries are already used up, Kozuka suggests—a suggestion, not an order—attacking Lubang township, to acquire more.

"Kozuka," comes Onoda's crushing rebuttal, "you are my leader today, but we can't attack Lubang. We would have to cross several kilometers of open flat ground, and Lubang has by my assessment eight hundred inhabitants. Probably more."

"Sorry," gulps Kozuka. "Well, it was just an idea."

Lubang, South Coast

1971

I n a well-disguised hiding place on the fringe of the steeply rising forest, Onoda and Kozuka are guzzling mangoes and pineapples. Kozuka is cheerful. "Pineapple season is the best season. Better than water buffalo season, and better than the time of the rice harvest."

"We have been here for two days now," cautions Onoda, "we should know how dangerous that is. Tomorrow we must get moving again, and this time follow the ribbon backward, Wakayama tributary, Looc Outlook, Hill 500, then Snake Mountain."

After darkness falls, the men head down to the shore to catch crabs. Afterward, Onoda lies on his back while Kozuka is on guard. Onoda spots something out of the ordinary with his field glasses. He checks with Kozuka that there is no prospect of danger, then gets him to come over. "There, at the bottom of the Great Dragon, something moving. You can see it with the naked eye even, the field glasses are not much good anymore."

Kozuka strains to see.

"To the left of the bottom gleaming star is another star that is moving rapidly from North to South."

Now Kozuka has it. "A very high-flying airplane?" he hazards.

"That was my first thought."

"Or a comet," wonders Kozuka.

"No. There is no tail, and we cannot see comets move with the naked eye."

"Odd." Kozuka tries with the field glasses, but they bring no improvement.

But Onoda is convinced. "Do you notice that its trajectory is precisely North to South?"

Kozuka nods.

"I saw this same star last night. It disappeared in the South, and then turned up again in the North about seventy minutes later but in a different place, as though it was following a regular orbit. But always flying exactly over both Poles. It can't be a comet or a high-flying airplane—no planes fly that high, or that fast. We can forget about meteors. There's a regularity in the movement that I wish I could account for."

The phenomenon preoccupies Onoda for weeks. He tests out all sorts of hypotheses only to reject them again. In the end he's left with a technical explanation that doubles as strategic thought. He explains it to Kozuka. "I'm certain that it is some man-made object, flying many times higher than an airplane, far outside the earth's atmosphere. The object is orbiting around our planet."

"Why?" asks Kozuka.

"It has a military function. My theory is as follows: I am convinced that it is possible to send an object into orbit, but to do so requires an extraordinary velocity such as can only be achieved by an extraordinary amount of fuel. I tried to work out how much and came to an amount that would correspond to an entire trainload of fuel to send just one kilogram of mass into orbit. And we must imagine many trainloads of fuel, because the object is of some size, otherwise we would hardly be able to see it with the naked eye."

"That's so much," marvels Kozuka.

Onoda raises his closed fist. "And why does the object navigate over both Poles, and at an even speed? Each revolution of the earth takes it a little more than one hour, an incredible speed."

Kozuka tries to keep up: "And why over the North and South Poles?"

Onoda picks up a straight twig and clasps it vertically in his fist, so that a little sticks out underneath and on top. "Imagine this is the axis of the earth."

He slowly turns his fist. "The object flies over the South Pole, is gone from sight, reappears over the North Pole, and carries on spinning. Now, this is the critical idea: with each rotation, the earth has turned a little farther so that each time, the object traces its course over a different segment of the earth. Like an orange, when you peel it and you see the segments. If it is forever flying from Pole to Pole, the object will by and by have a view of the whole planet, segment by segment."

"And what would be the good of that?" asks Kozuka.

"War, of course. War," Onoda replies confidently. "To build such an object is an extraordinarily complicated undertaking and would cost so much money that it can only be for some military purpose. It could be a viewing platform for the entire planet, segment by segment, or it could be a colossal bomb. It could be detonated at will over any place in the world. One could drop it on Antarctica or Mexico or even here, on our Lubang. No place on earth is safe any longer."

Soon after, the men make another discovery, much more prosaic this time, on their jungle footpath near 500: it is a

Filipino magazine torn to pieces. As Onoda cautiously flicks at the tattered remnant with the tip of his newly acquired machete—he is loath to touch the pages themselves—the two men see pornographic pictures. Strangely coiled naked bodies, performing unchaste acts in groups, in hopeless configurations. Kozuka had no objection to taking the scrap with them, but Onoda lets it lie where he saw it, lest the enemy, who had left it out as bait, understand that they had passed this way.

Lubang, Hill 500

1971

From inside a tangled bush, Onoda and Kozuka view strange developments on the bare summit. A provisional road has been laid through the jungle to the peak. Trucks, workers in hard hats, a troop of surveyors, two caravans placed side by side evidently constituting a temporary planning center. The most striking element is a luminous yellow Caterpillar earth mover from the United States. Away in the distance piled-up clouds are twitching with silent lightnings. Kozuka speculates on the construction of a very large artillery base, but what are the objectives within reach of guns located up here? And where are the soldiers to protect the workers? Through his wrecked field glasses, Onoda scopes out the terrain farther down, and discovers a troop of about fifty Filipino soldiers advancing slowly in an extended file toward the edge of the jungle. A soldier every couple of yards or so indicating to Onoda that this is no truly effective military maneuver; in the actual jungle they would have to be much closer together. Such a battue could only be effective with a thousand men along an entire kilometer. In all his time resisting, Onoda has yet to see sniffer dogs in use, and even sniffer dogs wouldn't stand a chance against armed men. You can only catch unarmed men with dogs, and the Philippine Army seems to have grasped that. As far as Onoda can see, the ineffectual parallel formation is just one more sign that the soldiers are too afraid to enter the jungle.

The two men are spending ever more of their time on the repair and patching up of their equipment. The humidity gnaws at everything, everything rots, frays, crumbles. When they do their weekly laundry in safety, it starts to rain, and they have to stash their half-dry clothing in a plastic sack. It rains the next day, and the next, and by the time it's dry again and sunny, they find their plastic sack pumped up like a rubber balloon about to burst. Everything in it is white and full of fine threads, it resembles a cloud of sugar candy from a children's fair, but what it is is a mold that has proliferated wildly.

Onoda is working on his pants, which he wants to patch with some material that in color at any rate bears some resemblance to the material of his original uniform. Kozuka meanwhile is weaving a rattan net that he wants to affix to the top of his rucksack.

"Why," he asks, "does the Lieutenant insist on having it the same color as his uniform? Why does it have to look proper?"

"Are we soldiers or tramps?" Onoda replies crossly.

The sound of a small airplane startles them, it appears to be circling. They run cautiously to a place where they can see better. The single-engine plane flies in slow loops, then one of the side doors is removed and replaced by a large loudspeaker.

"Lieutenant Onoda," says a voice in Japanese, "Private Kozuka, this is an appeal to you"—but then it takes a few more loops before the men have heard the entire message—"an appeal to you from the President. Come out of your hiding place, you are assured of an amnesty."

"Nonsense, that's another trap," Onoda declares. "Why send a whole battalion of men against us at the same time?"

Kozuka has doubts of his own. "President? President of what? Of the Philippines? And if so, then what about America? Or does he mean the President of the USA?"

The building site on Hill 500 seems to suggest some great bonding between the warring Americans and the Filipinos.

Lubang, Jungle Footpath

October 19, 1972

On the track once more, this time going backward. Onoda stops suddenly because the bird chatter has stopped. He dives into the thick foliage, Kozuka hides beside him. They see something silvery shimmering on the path. It seems to be a bit of tinfoil, like the scrap they found the other week, with a few crumbs of chocolate on it. Kozuka pulls himself up to make an inspection.

"Wait," whispers Onoda, but Kozuka is already out of cover. The tinfoil starts fluttering in his direction, as though an explosion had occurred, but it is gunfire. Shouts, wild movements, bullets shredding leaves. Then silence. Kozuka is standing in the middle of the path.

"Chest," he says calmly, as though talking to himself, "It's my chest."

His breath comes whistling, blood bubbles up at his mouth, and he flops down face forward.

Lubang

From late 1972

Onoda, for the next two years or few moments, is an ambulating piece of the jungle. On one occasion, sensing he can no longer get out of the way of a jogging column of Filipino soldiers, he hurriedly buries himself in foliage, sprinkles leaves over himself at the last seconds. In his haste, a straggler steps on his hand without noticing.

A campfire. Crickets. Mosquitoes. Rain and rain. Onoda is feeling meditative. He breaks off mussels from the rocks on the stony West coast. He lights a fire in the manner of the loggers, he leaves no trace behind. He thinks he has been forgotten, but one day he sees some men below Looc Overlook. One of them is carrying a loudspeaker on his back like a rucksack, his face is obscured from sight as he walks down the hill. The voice calls out in Japanese: "This is your brother, this is your brother. I am your brother Toishi."

Onoda goes rigid.

"Hiroo, my brother," calls the voice, "listen to me."

Onoda seems without emotion, his inside is stone. The unimaginable cannot be.

"My brother, come out wherever you are, come out, come out." The voice recedes into the distance, can hardly be heard.

Onoda strains everything in himself to follow it.

"I will sing a song now," calls the distant voice, "Hiroo, my brother, do you remember the song we used to sing at cherry blossom time?"

Onoda just catches the opening bar of the song, thereafter the jungle draws the voice into itself.

"See the falling blossoms, they are the souls of the dead, they sail through the air . . ."

What was that? Was that actually his brother, or some hazy chimera? Onoda is unable to account for the event in the structures of his belief. He is forced to live with the contradiction. In case it truly was his brother, why does he hear the voice for weeks and all over the island? The answer draws him in ever more powerfully: if that was his brother out with a search party, then he was letting him know, so to speak in a secret code, that the men were actually tasked with exploring every nook and cranny of Lubang to make a detailed topo-graphical survey for improved maps to facilitate the imminent reconquest of the island by the Imperial Army. Truth comes with hidden codes, or else the codes are unpredictably en-riched with reality, like the veins of ore in rock.

At this point, time stops still for weeks. Or rather, it doesn't stop, it simply no longer occurs. Then it hurries, leaps over weeks and months in the moment it takes a breeze to stir the leaves. Onoda goes around like a sleepwalker, but even that is not a true impression. He harbors two natures. Onoda goes around alertly, sees everything, hears everything. He is al-ways prepared. But he is not allowed to merely be jungle, be a part of nature. He is apart and a part. He must remind the populace in Lubang of his mission, so he steps out into the open on the northern plain outside Lubang township, and fires a few shots into the air. There is no one there. He has no need to take more supplies. He just wants to make himself heard.

Lubang, Wakayama Tributary

A Japanese flag is flapping over a large tent. Large enough for a man to stand up inside it. Beside it is Suzuki's smaller tent. Onoda is well hidden by the rushlike grass at the confluence of the two streams. He is motionless. Nothing, no Filipino soldiers, no reporters, there is clearly no ambush. Suzuki comes crawling out of his tent, and starts brushing his teeth, he is almost exactly above Onoda, whom he has not seen. "Don't move," says Onoda calmly, aiming his rifle at the back of Suzuki's head.

"Onoda," says Suzuki, "Hiroo Onoda."

"You have kept your word. Turn around."

"I have come with your commanding officer from Tokyo,"

says Suzuki, speaking into the mouth of the rifle, "Major Taniguchi."

"And otherwise?"

"No one else. A detachment of the Philippine elite Army Corps is expecting you on Hill 500."

"Armed?" asks Onoda.

"Yes, but only to salute you as a guard of honor."

"Where is my commanding officer?" Onoda is cautious. "I must assume there is some trap."

"Major," calls Suzuki, "would you kindly step outside. Lieutenant Onoda is here."

But the Major doesn't emerge, he hasn't got his boots on yet. Onoda stands and waits beside the mouth of the large tent. Within, hands fiddle with the opening. Taniguchi steps out, an old man, white haired and stooped, eighty-eight years old.

"Lieutenant," he says, "I recognize you. You have become a grown man."

Onoda salutes, takes two steps back, and presents arms.

"Do you recognize me?" asks Taniguchi.

"Yes, sir." Onoda tautens.

"I have new orders for you from the Ministry of Defense." Taniguchi is not in uniform, just an army shirt and the peaked cap of the Special Forces. He holds a piece of paper in his extended hands and reads from it. "In accordance with the Emperor's instructions, the Fourteenth Army and all other Japanese units have ceased all forms of combat. Units under the command of the Special Forces are hereby to cease hostilities forthwith. They are to place themselves under the command of the Philippine forces, and follow their instructions."

Onoda is quite impassive. He salutes.

"Lieutenant, your war is over." Because Onoda has gone rigid, Taniguchi now asks him in a kindly tone of voice: "Lieutenant, are you all right?"

Onoda's empty face betrays nothing, he seems turned to stone. Impassively, he replies: "Sir, there is a tempest raging within me."

"Lieutenant, at ease," says Taniguchi. "For form's sake, I must add that this command is valid as of now, oh-eight hundred hours, March 9, 1974."

Onoda suddenly drops to the floor, as though sapped to the back of the knees. The Major is disconcerted. "What is the matter, Lieutenant?" But Onoda is incapable of speech.

"Won't you say something," murmurs Taniguchi.

"If today is March 9," says Onoda incredulously, then I'm five days behind with my reckoning."

"You are twenty-nine years behind," Taniguchi corrects him.

On the way up to Hill 500, Onoda asks for leave to make a detour. He wants to fetch his sword from its hiding place in the tree hollow. His sword is in excellent condition, without a trace of rust. The sun gleams on the sheath. Until the very last moment, Onoda is later to confide, he has hoped that the Major will turn to him and tell him that this has all been a bit of theater, they had merely wanted to test his dependability.

Lubang, Hill 500

The bare hilltop has changed. The newly built radar station is taking shape. An elite unit of the Philippine Army is on parade. Taniguchi is first to step out into the open, followed by Onoda. An officer barks an order, and the unit presents arms. Onoda takes the inspection, mechanically, as though all this could only be an illusion. At the end of the line stands the General in overall command of the Philippine armed forces. Onoda steps up to him, salutes, surrenders his rifle. Then he hands over his sword as well, in both extended hands, but the general gives it back to him immediately. "The true samurai keeps his sword," he says. Onoda has long felt incapable of emotion, but later he will admit that inside everything in him was bawling.

And then this: shortly after Onoda's return to Japan, Norio Suzuki undertook his expedition to the Himalayas to find the yeti, as he had intended. At the foot of Dhaulagiri, he is struck by an avalanche and killed. Hiroo Onoda straightaway flew from Japan to Nepal. Accompanied by a Sherpa, he set off on the three-week trek and climbed to a height of five thousand meters, to the majestic southern flank of the eight-thousand-meter peak. At the place where Suzuki lay buried, the Sherpas had built a cairn. Onoda's bearer set down his rucksack. "This is the grave here." Onoda had the sensation of vast fists coming down upon him from the heavens, as though the infinite nature of the snowy peaks, the glaciers, the abysms would rip him in two. Onoda stepped up to the cairn. The only trace of the life that had been was a fluttering prayer flag. As impassive as everything around him, Onoda stood to attention. The clouds parted briefly, a shy glimpse of sunlight. No earthquake, no thunderbolt. Silence.

After Onoda had surrendered to the Philippine forces, he was taken by helicopter to Manila. Ferdinand Marcos, newly installed as President and still ruling by martial law, took the opportunity of having the surrender of the sword reenacted as a media spectacle. He, too, returned the sword right away. On his instructions, Onoda had put on his tattered uniform, even though he had been given a new suit of civilian clothes on Lubang. Marcos promulgated an amnesty for Onoda on the grounds that all these years he had been an enemy combatant. The people of Lubang themselves had taken Onoda for some sort of enemy agent. Years later, he went back there for a visit, and was well received by the locals. But the matter of those he had killed among the population never quite went away.

When news of the end of Lieutenant Onoda's solitary campaign reached Japan, the hearts of an entire nation stood still.

For his part, Onoda, greeted by a media scrum, was deeply distressed by the materialism of postwar Japanese society. To him, it was as though Japan had lost its soul. The Prime Minister wanted to receive him at once, but Onoda refused. He wanted first to meet the families of his fallen comrades. Later, he moved to Brazil, where his older brother, Tadao, had immigrated, cleared jungle in the remoteness of Mato Grosso do Sul, and started his own cattle ranch. He spent part of each year in his homeland, where he started the Onoda Nature School, a private establishment at which during the summer months he instructed camps of schoolchildren in survival techniques. Onoda married two years after his return. He had no children. He died in Tokyo at the age of ninety-one.

Onoda long refused to accept soldier's pay for his twenty-eight years. Only when pressed by his family did he finally accept the money, donating it right away to the Yasukuni Shrine. There, from the mid-nineteenth century, the names of the now 2.5 million people who had lost their lives for the fatherland were kept. (Strangely, also the names of some of their domestic animals.) The shrine is a somewhat controversial institution because it also houses the names of about a thousand convicted war criminals. At first, I hesitated to follow Onoda's invitation. He wanted to show me the remnants of his tattered uniform, which was kept there. As Onoda had been officially declared dead in 1959, there had been no signs of life from him for a long time, and it was assumed that he had died in the same ambush in which Shimada had been killed or that he had been mortally wounded like Kozuka, his name had been registered there for many years. It took two weeks of negotiations between Onoda and the head of the shrine before I was invited. I accepted the invitation, thinking who am I anyway to allow myself the luxury of such reservations, coming as I do from a country that has brought such horrors upon other countries and peoples. Onoda and I straightaway struck up a relationship. We found much common ground in our conversations because I had worked under difficult conditions in the jungle myself and could ask him questions that no one else asked him. On-oda had a song translated for me that he had kept singing to himself on Lubang, to keep his spirits up:

> *Quiet moon, I may look like a tramp or beggar,*
> *But you are witness to the glory of my soul.*

We knelt opposite the abbot in a long ceremony. Prayers were said, then the abbot turned to me. What he said was interpreted for me, but I have no memory of any of it. Finally, the abbot sent a monk from the room. He came back, carrying a flat carton secured with silk ribbon. Inside was Onoda's uniform, packed in crepe in the manner of precious garments. The crepe was carefully lifted aside, and there it was, the uniform that Onoda had worn for thirty years in the jungle, mended repeatedly. Onoda asked the abbot if he would let me take the uniform in my hands. I bowed, and the abbot laid it in my formally outstretched arms. The abbot exchanged a few words with Onoda, and encouraged me to unfold the uniform and to feel it. I did so with extreme care. As I did, I could feel something by the waistband. Onoda noticed, and nodded to me. I found a tiny brown glass bottle, of the kind that pharmacists use for medicines. It contained palm oil that Onoda himself had made. He hadn't realized that so many decades later, it was still hidden in his uniform. I felt a commotion beside me. Onoda hadn't got to his feet, something had pulled him upright. All those present, still on their knees, feeling the same stab to the heart, bowed down to him.

How could he have forgotten the bottle? Something real that was kept hidden somewhere apart from his memories. Often he had pondered whether the years in Lubang could have been years of sleepwalking, but if some concrete object that did not appear in his dreams suddenly materialized, then he couldn't have been in a dream after all. What marks the beginning of something palpable, and where is the memory of it? Why, he often asked himself, couldn't it be that his endless jungle march was an illusion? After all his millions of steps, he had understood that there was—there could be—no such thing as the present. Each step of the way was past, and each further step was future. The raised foot was past, the same foot placed in the mud in front of him still ahead. Where was there room for the present? Every centimeter of his foot going forward was the future, every centimeter behind was past. And so on, in smaller and smaller scale, in millimeters, in barely measurable fractions of millimeters. We think we live in the present, but there is no such thing. Am I walking, living, fighting? And then what about all those stretches when he had walked backward, to deceive the foe? Even his backward step was a step into the future.

The past could always be measured and described, but his memory had blurred events, sometimes bewilderingly mixed them up. Even a decade after Shimada's death he continued to see him in the jungle ahead. His memory had not extended its grace to the preservation of pain. (Otherwise women would hardly agree to bear more children after the pain of childbirth.) The future was always like a distorting but impenetrable fog lying over an unfamiliar landscape, though there was some knowledge of it. The day is ending. The sun will rise in the morning. The rainy season will begin in five months. And then the unexpected, the bolt from the blue: a bullet, like a seam of tracer in the gloaming. It will hit you, if you don't manage to turn aside at the last moment. The point that it would have struck, the solar plexus, is no longer where it was. The decay of his uniform is inevitable, but inevitabilities can still be avoided, or at least delayed. Each patch slows the disintegration, the wear, the rot. At the end it was still a uniform.

After the visit to the shrine we conversed in the park until nightfall. Was he then a sleepwalker, or was now, the present, something he had dreamed? He often racked his mind about the question on Lubang. There was no proof that when awake he was awake and no proof that when dreaming he was dreaming. The twilight of the world. Ants, when they stop, for some reason we don't understand, move their antennae. They have second sight. Crickets scream at the cosmos. Among the terrors of night was a horse with glowing eyes, smoking cigars. A saint left a deep imprint on the rock on which he slept. Elephants at night dream standing up. Fever dreams trundle the rock of night up the angry boiling mountains. The jungle bends and stretches like caterpillars walking, up-hill and down. The heron when cornered will attack the eyes of its pursuers. A crocodile ate a countess. The dead, when turned away from the sun, can be buried standing up. Three men on a horse, the saddle remains empty. The net of the sleeping fisherman continues to catch fish. A man who walks backward should also talk backward. Onoda backward is Adono. The heart of a hummingbird beats twenty times a second, twelve hundred times a minute; the silent Indios in the Mato Grosso do Sul believe they are alive twice. It is only among his cattle in the Mato Grosso that Onoda feels secure. His heart beats with their hearts, his breath comes and goes with theirs. When he is with them, he knows he is where he is. The night is over, and the swarms of fish know nothing.